BOMBER

BOMBER

PAUL DOWSWELL

BLOOMSBURY

LONDON NEW DELHI NEW YORK SYDNEY

Bloomsbury Publishing, London, New Delhi, New York and Sydney

First published in Great Britain in May 2015 by Bloomsbury Publishing Plc
50 Bedford Square, London WC1B 3DP

www.bloomsbury.com

Bloomsbury is a registered trademark of Bloomsbury Publishing Plc

A CIP catalogue record for this book is available from the British Library

ISBN 978 1 4088 5849 3

Typeset by RefineCatch Limited, Bungay, Suffolk
Printed and bound in Great Britain by CPI Group (UK) Ltd, Croydon CR0 4YY

1 3 5 7 9 10 8 6 4 2

To Ele Fountain – good egg extraordinaire.
And also
My friends J., M., T. and J. Ward

CHAPTER 1

Kirkstead, East Anglia, England, August 17th, 1943

Harry Friedman had been in England less than half an hour when the bomb group he was joining returned to Kirkstead. That was the moment Harry realised volunteering for the air force would probably cost him his life.

The day had started well, and Harry and the crew of the *Macey May* had arrived at their new airbase in good spirits, despite the dreary weather that greeted them when their B-17 bomber descended through the clouds.

They had never made such a long flight before and seeing endless blue sea stretching below had fired Harry's imagination. It made him think of the early seafarers he'd read about at school and what they must have thought when they were all alone in a great ocean, with only the edge of the world to fall off. When they spotted Iceland looming in the distance, he felt like an excited kid. Their navigator, Warren Cain, had directed them all the way from Newfoundland safely across that great void and landed them exactly on time to refuel for the last leg of their journey.

1

Iceland had looked extraordinary from the air and it did on the ground too, like something from the time of the dinosaurs, all craggy black rock and steaming geysers. There were volcanoes there, but they seemed to be asleep when Harry's crew passed through. He couldn't believe all these things he was seeing. He thought about his friends back in Brooklyn, and all the tales he'd have to tell them when he got back.

The refuel took about an hour and a cold wind was blowing in from the north, so they had all been glad to get back on board the *Macey May* and set off southward towards Britain, although he'd heard the British weather could be pretty unfriendly too.

By the time the B-17 touched down at Kirkstead, Harry was desperate to get off the plane, stretch his legs, and get away from the deafening drone of those four Wright Cyclone engines. Yet, despite its duration, it had been an easy flight – ten thousand feet most of the way. No need for oxygen or cumbersome flying suits.

There was a frustrating twenty-minute wait on the runway, then Captain Bob Holberg's voice came over the interphone to tell them they had finally been given permission to proceed to their designated hardstand. Holberg parked the *Macey May* on the eastern edge of the newly built airbase, and that constant roar of engines ceased with a judder and a cough. The short silence that followed was pure bliss; now they could talk without shouting. One by one the crew wriggled out, either from the small rear exit or the hatch beneath the cockpit. Here they were – replacement crew for the 488th Bombardment Group, 236 Bombardment Squadron.

Harry looked down the aircraft's great silver length from its tail to the nose, admiring its graceful curves, and told himself how lucky he was to fly in such a beautiful machine. It was supposed to be one of the safest planes in the United States Army Air Force – as safe as any plane could be that was built to fight in a war. The B-17 was bristling with thirteen powerful machine guns. Of the ten men aboard, everyone apart from the two pilots operated these guns. No wonder they called it the Flying Fortress.

It had been hot inside the B-17. Now Harry found himself shivering as a thin wind ruffled his curly black hair.

'Welcome to England, boys.' Holberg came over. 'You cold, Sergeant?' he said.

Harry nodded.

'If it's like this in August, just think what it'll be like in January!'

The crew looked glum, then tail gunner Jim Corrales said, 'Cheer up, fellas. We might all be dead by then.'

They laughed uneasily. Harry noticed Holberg giving Corrales a disapproving glance, but Harry didn't mind the tail gunner. He always made them laugh. It was good for 'morale' – a word Harry had never heard before he joined the USAAF. Someone back at the training camp canteen had told him it meant 'the will to keep on fighting when those around you are being killed by the truckload'.

Harry looked around the flat landscape. He was a city boy and had rarely left New York before he'd enlisted. Even though they'd just spent a gruelling few months training in the flatlands of Nebraska, he still wasn't used to an endless low horizon, where you could see for miles in all directions.

A jeep arrived at the hardstand to take them to their barracks. As they clambered aboard, Howard Bortz, the plane's bombardier, pulled Corrales from one of the back seats. 'Officers in the seats,' he said with a smile that didn't reach his eyes.

Corrales shrugged and clung to the side, like the other non-commissioned boys. All the gunners, and Clifford Skaggs on the radio, were sergeants.

The distant hum of aero-engines drifted over the airfield. 'They're back,' said the driver, a corporal with a strong Tennessee accent. 'We gotta wait here a while.'

They got off the jeep and stood scouring the eastern sky. Curtis Stearley, Holberg's co-pilot, passed around a packet of cigarettes. They all took one. It was a crew tradition after every flight.

Harry wasn't sure he liked Stearley. He was a tall Texan, with darkly handsome features, not unlike the Hollywood film star Clark Gable. Stearley cultivated the resemblance and had even grown a similar moustache. When the crew had gone out carousing, in a break from their long months in training, Harry had noticed girls seemed to fall for his easy charm. Harry smiled to himself. Maybe he was just jealous.

4

'Where they been?' Holberg asked the jeep driver.

The driver looked uncertain and Harry imagined he could almost see him thinking. Wasn't this classified information? The sort you weren't meant to discuss. But then, the bomb group had been there and dropped their bombs, so it couldn't be a secret any longer.

'Schweinfurt,' said the corporal. 'We heard it's been a rough one.'

The leading B-17 was now visible in the sky, getting bigger by the second. It made a perfect landing along the main runway and swiftly taxied over to the hardstands on the western edge. At once the air was full of noise and the acrid smell of aviation exhaust. B-17s continued to land in a steady procession and Harry could see some of them had been shot up pretty bad: a tail with struts beneath its metal fabric bare to the world; a feathered propeller and a blackened engine; a gaping hole in a fuselage.

One B-17 arrived trailing smoke from the outside right engine and fired a red flare as it approached the runway. Harry watched the smoking curve of the flare and instantly understood its meaning. There were badly injured men on board. It was the signal for ambulance crews to attend the stricken aircraft.

The B-17 touched down with a squeal of brakes, bouncing back into the air twice before it settled on to the ground and came to a halt at the very far end of the runway. Harry realised not one of his own crew had moved or spoken as the bomber made its descent. Now they were cheering.

Another bomber followed. This one too was trailing smoke from a left engine, but as it grew nearer they could see the inside right engine had also stopped. 'These things can land on one engine,' said Holberg, voicing everyone's concern, 'so he should be OK with two . . .'

He trailed off mid-sentence. This B-17 was now in its final approach and the landing gear had still not been lowered.

'Doesn't look good,' said Stearley, drawing hard on his cigarette.

Landing without wheels, flat on your belly, was just about the most dangerous way to come back to earth.

The bomber lurched unsteadily as it approached the main runway, the left wing dipping and almost touching the tarmac. Harry's eyes were drawn to the ball turret under the belly. He hoped the gunner had got out. The pilot tried to level off, but instead his plane tilted to the right side and the wing caught the ground. With an awful grinding of metal on concrete the Fortress lifted again, then landed hard, sliding down the runway almost sideways, sending up sparks. The right wing cracked between its two engines, and for a moment there was a spurt of aviation fuel, then a fireball so fierce they could feel it on their faces. The blazing bomber continued to hurtle along the runway at speed, getting nearer to the spot where their jeep was parked. Instinctively Harry and his companions started to sprint for the shelter of the trees that lined the eastern perimeter.

They heard another loud explosion and all dived to the ground. A few seconds later, debris of all shapes and sizes rained down around them. Harry looked back to see a great flaming pyre, maybe a hundred yards away. The heat was intense, and the crackle of the billowing orange and black flames almost drowned out the sirens of the approaching fire trucks.

The crew of the *Macey May* sat there on the concrete. Harry was glad no one else had tried to get up. He was sure his legs wouldn't carry him and he didn't want anyone else to know. He looked around at the *Macey May*. It seemed untouched by the explosion. That was good.

An ambulance arrived at the blazing wreckage just after the fire trucks. But the medics could see at once there was nothing for them to do. Ten lives had been lost in an instant. They returned to their little vehicle and sped off to another stricken aircraft. The firemen rapidly unrolled their fire hoses and began to spray the flaming wreck with bright white foam.

As the fire died down, the Tennessee corporal broke the horrified silence. 'Come on, boys, let's get you out to your barracks.'

The jeep was close to the fire, but not close enough to have sustained any damage. The crew of the *Macey May* picked their way through metal shards, coughing away the harsh stench of burning metal and fuel. As Harry approached the jeep he saw a tattered bundle of fabric lying on the tarmac. As he got nearer he realised it was the sleeve of a leather flying suit with a thick padded glove at one end. The fabric was charred and it didn't take him long to realise there was a severed arm inside it. He looked at his own sleeve and his own glove and turned around to spew his guts over the runway. No one said anything. His friend John Hill, the Fortress's left waist gunner, turned away and was sick as well.

CHAPTER 2

The barracks were more primitive than the accommodation the crew had had at their training camp in Nebraska and the gunnery school Harry had been sent to in Tennessee before he'd joined the crew of the *Macey May*. There was a single pot-bellied stove at the far end of the corrugated iron Nissen hut and bunks for twenty men.

All the non-coms had been placed in the same hut, so he would be with Corrales, the waist gunners, Hill and Dalinsky, and Skaggs, the radio operator. The commissioned men – the officers – were all sharing in another hut.

The place smelt of damp, woodsmoke and sweat. Each man already resident had tried to personalise his own little corner. Harry's eyes popped open at the sight of some of the pin-ups they'd plastered on the wall. All of a sudden he felt a very long way from his cosy family apartment in Brooklyn. He could still smell the greasy smoke from the runway explosion on his hair and clothes and longed to get under a shower to wash away the horror of the afternoon. But Holberg had said they had ten minutes to unpack before they had to report their arrival, then sit through a briefing on what awaited them.

They had several weeks of acclimatisation ahead of them – night flights, more training – before they would be considered combat-ready. Harry was grateful for that now. He had arrived over England feeling excited and ready to go. But that had vanished the second he saw that horrible yellow and black explosion – like an obscene rotting cauliflower. He realised then and there that Kirkstead might be the last place he would ever live, and his life might be over before he reached his eighteenth birthday.

For the first time he wondered if he had done the right thing in coming here. His buddies back in Brooklyn had been full of admiration when he'd told them he'd aced the air force induction interview and the recruiting officers hadn't batted an eyelid when he'd told them he was eighteen. He hadn't expected there'd be a problem. Harry had a stocky, muscular build. He spent most of his school vacations teaching local kids gymnastics and baseball. He had plenty of confidence too and people always assumed he was older than he was.

His parents were upset when he volunteered, but they knew there was no point trying to dissuade him. They'd all been hearing terrible things about what the Nazis were doing in the conquered territories. At first it was just rumours and the odd story in the newspapers. Then friends who had family in Germany, Poland and Czechoslovakia had told them letters had just stopped arriving. They were a pretty secular family, not even minding if Harry dated gentiles, but they were still Jews. And what they heard filled them with a mounting sense of dread and revulsion.

Harry had talked to Bortz, the bombardier, about this. He was Jewish too, and he had heard the same horror stories, and volunteered for the same reasons. Harry had always imagined there would be a bond between them, but Bortz was an uptight guy, who kept himself to himself.

'Come on, Harry, our ride's here. We gotta go.' John Hill's voice jolted him away from Brooklyn and back to Kirkstead. Harry slipped off the last of his flying gear and ran out to the jeep, clutching precariously to the side as it sped down a mud track to the main airfield buildings.

The briefing hall was just as makeshift as their Nissen hut and a thin draught whistled around their ankles. The linoleum on the floor was new but already scuffed, as were the flimsy trestle tables and chairs. Other crews joined them and they quickly realised these were men like them – just arrived from the States as replacement crews for the four squadrons that made up the bomb group at Kirkstead.

Holberg was sitting just behind Harry and deep in conversation with another captain. 'Worst raid yet,' he heard the man say. 'This squadron alone has lost four planes.'

Holberg swore under his breath – something which shocked Harry. His captain was a pretty upright guy – churchgoer. He even had a couple of kids. He wasn't the

11

swearing type, but then four planes was a third of a squadron.

Someone else chipped in. '303 over in Molesworth lost nine.'

Harry was horrified. Nine out of twelve planes. That was a massacre.

'What was it? Did they say?' asked Holberg. 'Flak? Fighters? Don't suppose they know yet . . .'

The conversation was interrupted by the arrival of the bomb group commander and they all stood abruptly to attention. The commander was a trim-looking man in his middle years, with razor-sharp creases in his trousers. He took off his peaked cap to reveal a thin crop of grey hair and addressed them all sternly.

'At ease, gentlemen, welcome to England. My name is Colonel Laurence H. Kittering. You join us at a critical time. Today my bomb group have just returned from Schweinfurt. Our target was the ball-bearing factory there, and early reports suggest they did a good job, but we've taken a bit of a beating.'

Most of the hall had heard about the losses already and a low mutter passed through the assembled crews at this last comment. Kittering ignored this and carried on speaking.

'I want to tell you why it was worth it. If we can wipe out their ball-bearing production plants, then the war will end a lot sooner. Now you've all heard that nursery rhyme, *For want of a nail?*' He paused, searching their faces for acknowledgement.

The men stared at him blankly. He seemed mildly irritated by their reaction.

'*For want of a nail the Kingdom was lost*,' he said. 'Well, that's what ball bearings are these days. They're the nail. Everything with a motor – tanks, trucks, planes – they use them. Artillery uses them, machine guns use them. Bombs and shells use them.'

He paused again. 'You knock out that ball-bearing plant in Schweinfurt, and another one the Krauts have down in Regensburg, and we're halfway to winning the war.'

Kittering spent the rest of his talk outlining the drills and exercises the new crews would be doing before they were ready for combat. Then he told them he expected them to behave themselves and be courteous to the British.

'The Limeys have been at war for four years. So, yes, everything looks a little shabby. The food is lousy, and there isn't much of it. Their clothes are a bit worn. Everything needs a coat of paint. But I don't want any of you boasting about how much better everything is Stateside. They don't want to hear it and neither do I. These people held out against the Krauts after they conquered the rest of Europe and they deserve our respect. Now, any questions?'

Jim Corrales put his hand up. 'How do the Limeys take to being called "Limeys", sir?'

There was stifled sniggering throughout the room. Kittering eyed him with suspicion, weighing up what he had said and wondering if he should put him on a charge. Harry marvelled at Jim's straight face. There wasn't an iota of mockery or insubordination in the way he had asked the question.

'They don't,' snapped the colonel. 'Next question.'

An officer stood up at the back of the room. 'Captain Wilbur Schwarz, sir. Is it true that this morning's raid on Schweinfurt cost twenty per cent of our mission aircraft? Can we expect subsequent missions to have a similar rate of attrition?'

The room erupted in concerned murmuring again, louder this time.

Colonel Kittering was not impressed. 'You'll all shut your mouths.' His voice cut across the hubbub and the room settled to a cowed silence. 'Rule number one at this airbase: you will not repeat idle gossip. Captain, you'll report to my office as soon as this meeting is over.'

There were no more questions after that. The men trooped out under the stern eye of the colonel, barely daring to speak. He saw Kittering grab Jim Corrales by the sleeve as he left the room and heard him say, 'One more crack like that in a briefing and I'll bust you down to private so fast you won't know your ass from a hole in the ground.'

Harry's crew all bunched together afterwards, outside the briefing hall. The day felt warmer and even held the promise of a beautiful late summer evening.

'Come on,' said Holberg. 'Let's go meet the ground crew.'

Sergeant Ernie Benik eyed the approaching new boys with trepidation. Most of them looked so young – kids fresh out of school or college, with their cock-of-the-walk strut. At once he felt the weight of his years. He was in his early forties – probably an old man in their eyes.

His previous crew had lasted a single mission. The one before that had managed five operations before they were shot out of the sky. And that was after three of them had been killed in action on the fourth trip – the ball turret and tail gunner, and the radio operator, all caught in a lethal salvo from a German fighter.

Ernie made it his business to retrieve the bodies from the cramped interior and he shuddered when he remembered he'd had to finish that job with a hose. Cannon shells, especially, made a terrible mess of flesh and blood. The haunted faces of the survivors as they and the replacements boarded the plane for that fifth mission had convinced Ernie that he'd never see them again. If he'd been a betting man he would have put money on it. But that would have been callous. And Ernie was not callous.

Some of the other crew chiefs had told him you shouldn't get too close to your aviators. Ernie didn't share this view. The United States Army Air Force was his family. He'd never married and had no kids. So he made a fuss of all the new boys.

He made a quick tally in his mind. The crew of the *Macey May* would be the fourth he'd looked after since he arrived in the late winter of '42. It was a tough life, and that bastard Colonel Kittering wasn't going to be offering them

15

any kindness. So why shouldn't he? The flyers usually had a wake-up orderly to get them up on mission days. Ernie made it his personal job to rouse his flyers.

As the men approached, Ernie called to his boys over the roar of the generator truck that was recharging the bomber's on-board power supply. 'Hey, fellas, knock that thing off and come and meet the new crew!'

The generator ground to a halt and a fresh silence settled around them. It was easy to see who was in charge of this bunch, and Ernie stepped forward to shake Holberg's hand, turning swiftly to do the same with the other flyboys who had gathered around him.

He waited for the final two of his team of oil-stained mechanics to clamber down from engine number three, which had its cover off, exposing its cylinders, pumps and gears to the elements.

'Meet the team,' said Ernie. Each man nodded as Benik introduced them. 'Lenny, Hal, Ray, Ted, Woody, Frank, Vic . . .'

'They're good guys,' Benik said to Holberg. 'You can count on them. Never let me down yet.'

Holberg introduced the crew of the *Macey May*, finishing up with LaFitte.

'And this is Second Lieutenant Ray LaFitte, our flight engineer.'

Benik shook LaFitte's hand. 'How'd she run over the Atlantic?'

'No problem at all,' LaFitte said.

'We'll do our best to keep it that way.'

Formalities over, Ernie said, 'Well, you fellas will want to get your bearings. Why don't you go stroll around the perimeter. You'll still be back in time for chow.'

The crew of the *Macey May* left. When they were out of earshot, Lenny said, 'Poor suckers. Hope they last longer than the previous lot.'

Ernie, who towered over all seven of his men, cuffed him lightly over the head. 'Hey, no sourpuss talk here. Who says these guys aren't gonna make it to twenty-five missions.'

Harry's crew wandered right to the edge of the airfield perimeter before their captain spoke. 'Nice guy, isn't he?'

They all murmured in agreement. How would anyone not like Ernie Benik?

'Maybe this place isn't so bad after all,' Holberg said, waving his arm towards the field before them. It looked beautiful in the soft, early-evening light. Two horses were grazing in the pasture beyond the hedgerow, and the nearby village looked impossibly picturesque. A church spire stood silhouetted against the sky, and there was a manor house and several cottages that wouldn't have looked out of place on a chocolate box. It was a world away from the teeming streets of Brooklyn. Harry was wondering how soon he might get the chance to explore outside the airbase when John Hill brought him swiftly back to reality with a question for Holberg.

'Excuse me for asking, Captain, but that thing Captain Schwarz said – about losing one in five of the bombers today –'

Holberg cut him off.

'Schwarz had no business raising it like that. The colonel was right to chew him out. It might be true, it might not. And even if it is, maybe most of those guys got out before they crashed. I want you all to put it out of your minds. All we can do is train the best we can and make sure we're among those crews that always do come back.'

The church clock chimed seven. 'We got an hour before the mess closes,' said Holberg. 'It's been a long day. I suggest you all hit the hay as soon as you can. But tomorrow evening, if we can get a pass out, I want us all to go find one of those Limey pubs.'

Harry liked Bob Holberg. He was like a favourite teacher or uncle. Holberg had actually been a teacher before he'd joined up. English had been his subject and he'd taught in a prep school in Connecticut. He'd told them they only needed to salute him when other officers were around. Other captains were far more formal with their crew – and would only be addressed by their rank and surname.

Harry had been training with the crew of the *Macey May* for four months now, and most of them were great guys. He was looking forward to trying out the local beer with them and getting to know a bit more about this country. So far he hadn't even heard a Brit speaking.

*   *   *

18

They arrived at the mess at the same time as the non-coms from another Fortress. The boys from *Carolina Peach* introduced themselves. Like Harry's crew, they were from all corners of the United States.

They had arrived late that afternoon and they too had seen the still-smouldering remains of the B-17 on the main runway.

'Beautiful evening though, ain't it, boys?' said the shortest airman among them, obviously keen to change the subject.

'You're the ball turret gunner, right?' said Harry, and put out his hand.

'Damn right! Charlie Gifford.' He had a really firm grip, the sort that hurt your hand. 'Takes one to know one.' Gifford smiled. He was several years older than Harry and a striking man, with blond hair and blue eyes – the perfect Aryan, if you believed that garbage the Nazis spouted about the 'master race'.

'You a volunteer?' he asked Harry, and from the way he said it, Harry got the feeling he suspected he was underage.

Harry nodded.

'Recruiting officer must have forgot his glasses the day he interviewed you.'

Harry tensed, but Gifford winked. 'Don't worry, I ain't about to go tell the group commander.'

All ten of them sat round the same table and ate an unappealing stew and some kind of sponge, with a tasteless white sauce with a skin like a plastic balloon and a lumpy, paste-like texture.

'I guess the USAAF isn't famous for its haute cuisine,' John Hill said. He had been training to be a chef in a New York hotel when he joined up.

'At least we ain't on the diet they got the Limeys on,' said Skaggs. 'I read they get one egg a week.'

Gifford was sitting next to Harry. 'This the posting you wanted?' he asked.

Harry shook his head. 'I was hoping to get some place out in the Pacific. See something different. Somewhere I'd never get the chance to see in civilian life.'

But Gifford scoffed. 'England's much better than some flyblow island in the Pacific, fighting the Japs.'

'Japs execute Allied pilots if they capture them,' chipped in another of the *Carolina Peach* boys.

Harry had heard about that too. A photo had been passed around in the mess hall at the training camp in Nebraska. There was a blindfolded Allied fighter pilot, kneeling down about to have his head chopped off by an officer with a samurai sword, while a crowd of Japanese soldiers looked on. Harry had felt a wave of nausea when he'd seen that. He couldn't imagine what it would feel like to be that young pilot, waiting for the fatal blow. Maybe England was better after all.

'Hey, Charlie, you see that doll on the *Yankee Doodle*?' called out another guy in his crew. 'She's buck naked, man!'

The *Macey May* had parked next to it when they had arrived. Their own nose illustration was more restrained. Corrales made the whole table laugh, telling the story of the *Macey May*'s nose art. Holberg had named his Fortress after his wife, and had been shocked to see the painting Stearley and Hill had done – a blonde girl with a Betty Grable hairdo, wearing nothing but a pair of red stilettos.

John Hill laughed. 'Captain made us put her in a red bathing suit when he saw it.'

After they'd eaten, the non-coms from the *Macey May* said a friendly farewell to the *Carolina Peach* boys and went for another stroll around their new home and watched the last of the sunset. It was magical, but it reminded Harry how fragile his link was to this beautiful world. He noticed Ralph Dalinsky cross himself and mouth a silent prayer and envied him. Harry didn't know what to think, but he found it hard to believe in a God looking over his creation if even half of what he'd heard about the Nazis was true.

It was almost dark when they returned to their hut. Jim Corrales turned on the light switch and they were shocked to see that half the room had been cleared out. All the cases and pin-ups and drying clothes that had been there this afternoon had gone. And the bunks had been stripped of their linen. The hut had been given a clean too and smelt of bleach.

'Sweet Jesus,' said Corrales. 'Those guys were standing here this morning, just like we are now. Then they flew to Schweinfurt and they're gone.'

'Maybe they moved to another hut?' said John. Everyone else just shook their heads.

It reminded Harry of the time he had spent in the Beth-El Hospital in Brooklyn with his elder brother, David, during the 1941 polio outbreak. His brother had been far sicker than him and was sent to another ward. When Harry went to see him the next morning, he found an empty bed laid out fresh and ready for the next patient. A sharp smell of bleach had hung in the air. Knowing at once that David was dead, Harry had fled in helpless tears. Every time he smelt it now it sent a shiver through his body.

They prepared for bed in silence, each man lost in his own thoughts. Harry stared at the bottom of the bunk above, wondering if he was ever going to get to sleep. He was too tired. And, he had worked it out, it was still only six o'clock in the evening over there in Brooklyn. He thought of his mom and dad. He had promised to write to them the minute he arrived in England, but he just wasn't in the mood. The day's events played out in his mind. It had been a real roller coaster. The joy of flying above the clouds. Relief when they had landed safely after such a long flight. The thrill of being in a strange new land. Horror at witnessing such a gruesome crash.

When Harry finally fell into a restless sleep his dreams were troubling. As a child he had read about the gods of ancient Greece and how they could cut the silver thread of life according to their whim and fancy. In his mind's eye he saw himself gliding like a bird through sunset clouds, suspended from that silver thread. At once he felt in terrible danger and woke with a start. His chest felt heavy; his mouth was dry. Outside, dim light peeped through the flimsy curtains. It felt cold and damp in the hut and he shut his eyes tight, dreading what the next few days would bring.

CHAPTER 3

August 20th, 1943

Three days after they arrived, Harry's crew had still not been allowed to leave the airbase. 'They think we'll run away!' said Jim Corrales. 'Go off to London and join a Limey circus! Beats this gig, that's for sure!'

On the second day at Kirkstead they had all attended escape classes as a crew. A crusty British officer, on loan from the RAF, introduced himself as Flight Lieutenant Bowman.

'It is extremely important that you bury your parachute as soon as you land,' he said, in clipped upper-class tones, just like a Hollywood Brit.

Dalinsky put up his hand. 'When do we get to try out the parachutes, sir?'

The flight lieutenant gave him a hard stare. 'When your aeroplane is on fire and you need to get out of it.'

A murmur of discontent went round the room. Holberg stood up, announcing his name and rank to let this guy know he wasn't going to be talked down to, and asked if he was serious. 'Do you mean to say we aren't trained on how to bail out from a plane?' he asked.

'You train on the ground,' said the flight lieutenant. 'You go through the bailing-out drill until you can do it blindfolded. All you have to remember is to pull that ripcord on your chute after you count to five. That way you'll be clear of the aircraft. Take it from me, you don't need training for that.

'And you need to ditch your uniform as soon as you make contact with friendly French or Dutch civilians,' continued Bowman. 'I think we can safely say there will be no friendly German civilians.'

He smiled at his little joke. Harry was still reeling from the news that there would be no proper parachute training. Surely it couldn't be that simple. How did you steer the thing or land?

'You must find civilian clothes as quickly as possible,' said Bowman. 'But it is essential you keep your identity discs.' He stopped and for a brief moment a look of distaste flashed across his face. 'I believe you call them "dog tags". If you're caught without "dog tags", the Germans might think you are a spy and that will prove fatal.'

To underline his point he said, 'Spies are shot if they are lucky, and tortured then shot if they are not so lucky.'

At first Harry had found it difficult to take this stuffed-shirt Brit seriously, but as the lecture progressed a cold chill settled in his guts. This was definitely not a game. It had never yet occurred to him that if they survived being shot down, they would face another terrifying ordeal on the ground.

25

'I urge you all to take the latest issue of a British newspaper with you when you go into combat. If you have a copy of *The Times* or the *Eastern Daily Press*, then you can prove to Fritz that you have just arrived.'

That, at least, seemed a pretty simple thing to do to stop you being shot.

After the lecture, they went off to have their photos taken. This, explained Bowman, was so they could carry passport-sized prints for fake identity cards. The photographer had a small selection of weather-beaten jumpers and jackets. 'You're supposed to be a French civilian. You can wear a beret too, if you really want to get into the role.'

The next day, the little passport-sized photographs arrived. 'Hey, Friedman, look at you.' Corrales ruffled his hair. 'You look like a little cherub.'

Harry batted away his hand. 'And you look like an axe murderer.'

He didn't like the guys teasing him about his age. He hadn't told any of them he was really seventeen, but he thought they probably knew. He told himself to forget about it. He was here now, and if anyone was going to stop him from flying, they would have done so by now.

They had another lecture later that morning, this time from the colonel. Kittering told them it had cost many thousands of dollars to train them, so it was their duty as loyal Americans to try to escape if they were shot down. Harry wanted to ask about parachute training, and how they were supposed to land, but he lost his nerve.

Sometimes you were made to feel like there were questions you just didn't ask.

After breakfast the following day, Holberg gathered them together in front of the *Macey May* and announced they would be making a high-altitude flight that morning. Most bombing raids were flown at twenty-five thousand feet, even thirty thousand. It was thought this great height would offer protection from German flak and fighters. That was higher than most of them had ever flown before, even in training. They were to report to the equipment store immediately to draw out oxygen masks and heated suits.

'You need to shave every morning you have a high-altitude flight,' said the instructor, after they'd collected their masks. 'If these masks leak, you won't get enough oxygen. You can easily pass out without even realising. And if no one else on the flight notices, they'll find you stone cold dead by the time they find out something's wrong.'

Harry felt a twinge in his gut and recalled mess-time conversations with other B-17 crews, warning them of the perils of high-altitude flying.

The masks were strange things – leather and canvas muzzles that attached to their leather flying caps, with a snaking tube that connected to their individual oxygen supplies. They took away your individuality, making you an anonymous sinister figure – like something out of a science-fiction movie, Harry thought.

Harry's high-altitude suit was a curious affair too. Over his vest and underpants he pulled on a heavy one-piece suit made of blue woollen fabric lined with heated wires. On top of that came heavy canvas trousers and shirt and a sheepskin-lined leather flying jacket.

He didn't like the idea of having that electricity right next to his underwear.

'You'll be grateful for it,' said Curtis Stearley, the co-pilot, who was standing by Harry in the equipment store. 'I had to do one or two high-altitude flights in training and it's pretty unpleasant that high up. Nothing like the trip we did over the Atlantic. And you'll be in that little ball, barely able to move to keep yourself from freezing. Look after that suit, Harry. It'll be a lifesaver.'

Not for the first time, Harry regretted the duty he had been assigned. He was the *Macey May*'s ball turret gunner. His own physiognomy had decided his fate. There was no volunteering. At five foot six, he was the shortest in the crew, and the ball turret needed a small man to squeeze in and operate it.

To begin with, Harry had been fascinated by his revolving Sperry turret with two powerful Browning machine guns, slung under the belly of the B-17, just behind the wings. But then he got his hands on the instruction manual and realised what a nightmare it was. Just climbing into the turret could kill him. If he didn't do it right, the turret might turn on its finely balanced rocker and snap him in half against the side of the aircraft. What made it even more difficult was that you only got into the turret once the plane had taken off, and you had to get out of it before you landed. He didn't like the idea of lowering himself in with ten thousand feet between him and the ground, and the aircraft shaking and jolting about.

The turret was as cramped as expected, especially in a heavy flying suit. But once you were in it, and had mastered the complex controls, there was no denying it was an amazing piece of machinery. You could swivel round 360 degrees at the push of a lever, and the whole thing rocked from 0 degrees level with the belly to 90 degrees straight down with equal ease. Early on in training, back in Nebraska, some of the gunners had dropped out, claiming being in the turret made them so nauseous they could not cope. But Harry had discovered he was unaffected by all that swivelling and dipping throughout the whole field of fire. Operating the gun excited him, despite its danger and discomfort.

What he couldn't shake off though was the thought of how awkward it would be to get out of that little ball if the B-17 was going down. There was no space for a parachute in there. And he could imagine how difficult it would be to get out when everyone else was abandoning the plane.

By ten o' clock that morning the crew had all clambered into their heavy flying gear and were ready to go. Holberg gathered them round, underneath the nose.

'You need to be on full alert throughout this flight,' he told them sternly. 'Sometimes German fighters pounce on bombers on training missions. They think we'll be easy meat. Combat rookies. So let's prove 'em wrong. You've all done your drills; you're all good shots.'

Then he softened. 'And I definitely don't want your folks getting a telegram telling them we were shot down over Cheshire or the Irish Sea.'

Like a football team before a game, before embarking they gathered together in a group hug.

'OK,' said Holberg, 'let's go,' and the crew dispersed to their various entry hatches.

'You could go hunting at the North Pole in this,' said John, as the rear gunners clambered into the narrow door just in front of the tail.

Dalinsky smiled. 'I'd feel a lot safer with a Browning than a harpoon.'

It was cumbersome moving around, but once the *Macey May* had taken off and Harry had clambered into his turret and plugged in his heated suit, he began to feel quite snug. It was a cloudless late summer day, and the blue sky and green land with its patchwork of fields and farms made for a stunning vista.

They climbed steadily, heading north-west towards the Isle of Arran, off the west coast of Scotland. That was to be their turning point and would provide them with a flight time similar to the bombing runs they would be expected to make over enemy territory.

After half an hour Holberg's voice came over the interphone. 'Ten thousand feet. Oxygen masks on. Keep watching the skies.'

30

Holberg never wasted a word when they were flying, although he was friendly enough on the ground. He instilled in them all the importance of saying only what needed to be said when they were airborne.

The four aero-engines screamed with the effort of lifting the heavy bomber up towards the edge of the stratosphere and as they climbed and the plane banked slightly in a turn Harry noticed how the sky above grew darker blue as they edged towards their maximum height of thirty-five thousand feet.

It was strange up there. Too high for birds and certainly no place for a human being. The cool, clean oxygen Harry was breathing kept his head clear and he maintained a steady watch, slowly rotating his turret through its 360 degrees. Sometimes it was difficult to keep up the watching, staring into infinite nothing. But Harry was keenly aware that this was the first flight they were making where they might meet with an enemy fighter. For the first time they were in danger of being killed in action.

He noticed a few wispy cirrus clouds drift by below and watched the engine exhausts leave four fluffy white trails against the blue sky as they ploughed through the stratosphere. Despite the cold and discomfort, he couldn't help feeling this was a magical place.

When they got back to Kirkstead, Holberg gathered his crew round and congratulated them on a successful flight. Then he announced he had got them all a day pass to

Kirkstead for tomorrow. There was a 'jumble sale' he told them, and a fête with a cake baking contest. It would be their first immersion into British life.

'Sir, what the hell's a jumble sale?' asked Jim Corrales.

'You better make sure you read your *Servicemen's Guide to Great Britain*,' said Holberg. 'I'm sure it'll all be "jolly nice".'

They all smirked, but Harry went back to his bunk and read that very manual. A jumble sale, it said in the glossary, was a rummage sale.

For the crew of the *Macey May*, Saturday morning had the makings of a perfect day. A crisp dawn, ham and eggs for breakfast, and a leisurely shower before they all assembled in their best dress uniform – the one they wore for parades and other formal ceremonies.

But that morning was also the bomb group's first mission since Schweinfurt. As Holberg and his crew strolled towards the village, they stopped to watch the active service crews take to the sky. The squadron was still under-strength from its usual twelve after the disaster of Schweinfurt, and they counted ten planes taking off. The *Macey May* crew weren't supposed to know, but it was no secret that this was a short mission over to the Charleroi steel plant in Belgium.

Ralph Dalinsky spoke to Holberg. 'It don't feel right, us going out to enjoy ourselves while the bomb group is off over enemy territory, sir.'

The captain just shook his head. 'We'll be up there with them soon enough, Sergeant, so just enjoy yourself while the sun is shining.'

Kirkstead was only a few minutes' walk from the base and they arrived to find a crowded church hall, full of bustling bargain hunters and the tables already half empty. Seeing Harry's disappointed face a stout elderly lady in a floral dress hooked her arm around his. 'Rule number one of jumble sales, young man: get there early. This one's been open for nearly an hour.'

She was the first English person who had spoken to him directly, and all of a sudden Harry felt tongue tied. He had expected the Brits to be frosty and polite, but she was just like his grandmother back in Brooklyn.

'Thanks for the advice, ma'am,' he said politely.

'Now, what are you looking for?' she asked with a twinkle in her eye. 'I'm on the committee. We can't buy things – people would say we earmarked all the best goods. But there's nothing to stop me helping you find something nice.'

Harry told her he was hoping to find some mementos for his mother and father. They fell into easy conversation, and Harry began to relax. His new friend introduced herself as Mrs Gooding and offered to show him around the fête. 'Everyone is so glad you boys are here with us,' she told him, patting him on the arm. 'The world was a frightening place when we were facing Hitler alone.'

They walked outside into a large field where trestle tables had been set up beneath the shade of several large oaks. One table contained a display of cakes and biscuits together with the names and addresses of those who had baked them. 'Look out,' said Mrs Gooding. 'Here comes trouble.'

A bird-like woman, of similar age to her, approached the table with a small entourage of other elderly ladies. 'She's the cake judge. Shows no mercy. The others in the WI are terrified of her.'

'Excuse me, ma'am – WI?' asked Harry with a tilt of his head.

'Women's Institute. It's an organisation for ladies who don't have anything better to do,' she said with a chuckle. 'I'm the local chairwoman.'

Harry and Mrs Gooding watched the judge from afar. Assisted by her entourage, she took minute slices from the offerings, tasted them and wiped her mouth with a little lace handkerchief. Then she wrote a small comment on each of the name tags attached to the cakes.

Harry was enjoying this immensely. It was just like observing a newly discovered tribe and their arcane rituals. His brother David, a lanky, bookish kid, had wanted to study anthropology at Columbia University and he had often told Harry about the rites and ceremonies of obscure South American or Micronesian tribes.

'We'll come back in a moment,' announced Mrs Gooding, and steered Harry over to the bring-and-buy stall. 'You might find something here,' she told him, gesturing to a table of ornaments – vases, glass animals and little statuettes. 'I must go and circulate.'

It was the perfect place and Harry quickly found a brass horse's head for his father and a little china tableau of a basket full of flowers for his mother. He was sure they'd love them.

'Let's see,' said the elderly gentleman on the stall, 'seeing as you're having the pair, let's say one and six.'

Harry got out his wallet and pulled out two pound notes, hoping the man would be honest with his change. He was aware that this was a fortune for two small ornaments, but he was sure they were valuable. Besides, there was little else to spend his money on.

The man was looking astonished. 'Blimey, I can't change that. Haven't you got any coins on you?'

'What seems to be the problem, Mr Reece?' It was Mrs Gooding, come to rescue Harry. 'One and six,' she explained 'One shilling and sixpence. Put all that money away, if you don't mind.' She reached into her pocket and paid the stallholder.

'You can pay me back later,' she said to Harry. 'Now I'd like to buy one of those cakes.' She directed him over to the cake stall.

On the way there John Hill called over. 'Hey, Harry, who's your lady friend?'

'You're an impertinent young man,' said Mrs Gooding with a twinkle in her eye. Harry could tell she wasn't really offended.

'We're off to buy a cake. You coming to join us?' said Harry, quickly introducing his friend to Mrs Gooding.

She looked him up and down and smiled. 'Come and observe the British art of cake judging. It's not for the faint-hearted.'

The judging had finished and the table was surrounded

with a flock of women of all ages, keen to see what she had written. There was laughter and suppressed howls of outrage. John, Harry and Mrs Gooding began to read the judge's comments.

These are the worst scones I have ever tasted. 0/10

Texture fine, but too dry. 3/10

Sickly. 4/10

Lardy. 1/10

A fine balance of sweet and tart. 8/10

'I'll have that one, before someone else has it,' said Mrs Gooding, pointing to the plum cake that had met with the judge's approval.

'Now, why don't you both come home and help me eat the cake with a nice cup of tea?'

Mrs Gooding lived in a small white house close to the church hall and sat them down in her garden on a couple of deckchairs. She brought them tea and two generous slices of plum cake.

The cake was quite as delicious as the judge's comments had suggested and reminded Harry of the cakes you could buy at the deli at the end of his street. He felt a stab of homesickness. John was beginning to doze off in the early afternoon sun, so Harry carried their cups and plates back inside and kept Mrs Gooding company while she peeled potatoes for her evening meal.

'Grandma, there's a strange man in the garden! Have you been rounding up American airmen again?'

Harry turned around, startled. The voice belonged to a petite girl now standing in the kitchen doorway.

'Here's another one!' She gave him a winning smile, and put out a hand for him to shake. 'Tilly Tait,' she announced, and gave a little curtsy.

Harry guessed she was somewhere in her late teens. She had a shock of wavy blonde hair and a delicate pink complexion, and Harry thought she was the prettiest girl he'd ever seen.

For the second time that afternoon he was lost for words, and to his horror he began to blush.

'Let me guess,' she said. 'You're a new arrival at Kirkstead.'

'Yes, ma'am,' he managed to say, and gave her an awkward salute. 'Sergeant Harry Friedman, United States Army Air Force.' Then his mind went completely blank. He wanted to tell her how much he liked her green dress, but he thought that would be too corny.

Mrs Gooding came to the rescue. 'Tilly is my grand-daughter, as I'm sure you've guessed. She's staying with me.'

'Our house has been requisitioned for some of your top bods at the base,' Tilly said. 'Mum's working in London, Dad's off in the navy, so I'm here.'

John picked that moment to come in. Despite the fact he had only just woken up, John was a lot more self-assured, introducing himself and making small talk with an easy charm Harry envied.

'The cake was delicious, Mrs Goulding, thank you,' he

37

said. Harry felt pleased he'd got her name wrong. He didn't want Tilly to like him instead.

John spoke again. 'Come on, Harry. We've got to get back to the base.'

They said their goodbyes and Tilly gave John what Harry hoped was a polite but indifferent nod. Turning to him, she lit up with a bright smile. 'Goodbye, Harry. See you again.'

The sun still shone brightly in the sky, and they walked back down the country lanes in high spirits. 'She's a peach,' said John, 'and she likes you, you lucky son of a bitch!'

Harry could feel himself blushing again. He wasn't going to tell John, but he didn't know a great deal about girls.

The sound of aero-engines reached their ears. 'They're back,' said Harry, grateful for the opportunity to change the subject.

In moments the sky filled with the sound of returning bombers. No one crashed as they landed and they could see no flares from approaching aircraft indicating seriously wounded men in need of urgent treatment.

Ten had taken off that morning and a quick tally of the planes as they weaved round to take their positions in landing formation revealed all of them had returned.

John Hill squeezed Harry's elbow. 'Look at that! All of them made it back. Maybe we'll survive after all.'

CHAPTER 4

September 8th, 1943

As August turned to September, their time in training began to drag. There was a seemingly endless succession of lectures on aircraft identification, gunnery tactics, formation flying and the intricacies of the B-17's hydraulic and electrical systems. Harry could see how it was all supposed to be useful, but he was beginning to think his brain couldn't take any more.

Harry also began to realise that there were certain men it was best to avoid. They were easy enough to spot – the shaky ones with frightened eyes; and the ones who seemed to delight in putting the wind up the new boys – like the two older guys, Gus and Lenny, who sat with Harry and John one time in the mess.

They were in their mid-twenties maybe, both gunners, recently transferred from Rattlesden. They spent the whole meal swapping gory stories about crews who had been killed on missions.

'That Fort that crashed here back from Schweinfurt, the one that landed with its wheels up,' Lenny said. 'Heard the belly turret gunner got trapped in that little ball . . .'

John interrupted. 'Hey, fellas, leave it, will you? We saw that plane crash as soon as we got here.'

'You a ball turret gunner?' Gus asked Harry with a smirk.

He guessed they probably knew his position on the *Macey May* and were just trying to make him crack. He tried not to let them bother him, but what he'd heard put him off his food.

'Strawberry jelly,' Lenny said, with added sound effects to drive the point home. 'Ya wouldn't get me in one of them ball turrets.'

Harry and John got up to leave soon afterwards. As they walked back to their hut, Harry felt a wave of despair as he thought about how small his chances of survival actually were. 'Do you think anyone does their twenty-five missions?'

'Those creeps in the mess got to you, didn't they?' John said, and put a hand on Harry's shoulder. 'Not everybody dies in a bomber that goes down – don't ever forget that, Harry. They parachute out. Why d'you think they give us those talks about escaping? It happens all the time.'

Their Nissen hut was still half empty, which suited them. It would not be filling up until more new crews arrived. For the moment, they had nearly as much space as the officers. But Harry was spooked by the empty beds on the other side of the aisle. He realised the bunk he now lay in had been previously been occupied by a man who was now most likely dead.

He could imagine his predecessor, a young man from Idaho, or San Francisco, or Maine, staring at the underside of the bunk above, a stranger in a strange land, having the same anxious nights as him. Had that guy wondered what fate awaited him? You'd have to be made of stone not to. He wondered whether he'd been killed by flak or cannon fire from a Nazi Messerschmitt, or that newer one, the Focke-Wulf ... or maybe he'd been trapped in a burning Fortress as it plunged to the ground. You only died once, but as an aviator there were a thousand ways to die.

As they got ready for bed, John tried to lighten the mood. 'Tell you what, boys, when all this is over, I'll cook you all a coq au vin at the fancy restaurant I'm gonna be workin' in.'

'After the garbage they give us in the chow hall, we're gonna be ready for it,' said Dalinsky.

Corrales had come in from the washroom, carrying a towel under his arm. 'Hey, Hill – don't talk crap. You're Irish, ain'tcha? They have the worst food in the world, apart from the Limeys!'

John smiled. 'Bet you I cook a better chilli than your mama!'

'Hill, everyone cooks a better chilli than my mama.'

But Harry was not in the mood to join in the joshing with his buddies. As he tried to fall asleep he kept thinking about what John had said about parachuting down. You'd have an uncertain future in the hands of the Krauts. But 'uncertain' was better than dead. Dead was never having another conversation with your loved ones and friends, never seeing another sunset ... He'd understood that when David had died.

41

*   *   *

As their fourth weekend at Kirkstead approached, Holberg told them all to rest on the forthcoming Sunday because that evening they would be going on a night-flying exercise.

It was overcast with a definite chill in the air, the sort of day that held the promise of dreary autumn. Harry decided that was a day he would write home.

As he sat staring at the blank sheet of paper before him he couldn't quite believe the situation he found himself in – he couldn't guarantee he would even see his eighteenth birthday that October, never mind the coming Christmas.

He knew he couldn't write these things in a letter to his mom and dad. What would they think if he told them he was convinced he would be killed in the next few weeks? They were worried enough about him going off to fight already. He also knew that the crew's letters all went through the communications officer and were all read and censored.

He picked up a pencil and began to write.

Dear Mom and Dad,
    You wouldn't believe what happened the other week . . .
we all went down to this pretty little village straight out of
the movies to a rummage sale and I bought you a couple
of cute little treasures, which I look forward to giving to you.

Even as he wrote it he felt a twinge of unease. Wasn't that tempting fate?

He rubbed out *I look forward to giving to you* and wrote *will look good on the fireplace*, then racked his brains trying to think of something else to say . . .

This nice old lady called Mrs Gooding took me under her wing and helped me out with the Limey money. Then she took me and John Hill back to her house for cake and tea. We met her granddaughter Tilly, who is staying with her for the duration of the war. She was really sweet.

They're not all sweet though, the English. If they fight Hitler as fiercely as their old ladies judge their cake baking contests, then we're going to win this war easy!

Please don't worry about me. My crew are all really good buddies and I feel safe up there in the sky in our Flying Fortress.

Every day brings new excitement and amazing experiences. We're all looking forward to having a chance to get back at Hitler. I'm taking everything one day at a time, wondering what tomorrow will have in store.

Your loving son
Harry

He was quite pleased with that. He hoped he'd make them smile and stop them worrying about him for a brief time at least. He knew that as their only remaining son they must be terrified of losing him too.

Harry had always felt guilty about his brother and wondered if he had been responsible for his death. The

43

two of them had been out in Manhattan in the high summer of 1941 – on a trip to the Museum of Natural History. It had been a few months before Pearl Harbor. Harry had been fifteen, David sixteen. On the subway there, David had started to feel ill and Harry had cajoled him into staying with him. They had been on their way to see some new exhibits in the Museum's Akeley Hall of African Mammals. They had both been talking about it all week and Harry didn't want to miss it.

Throughout their childhood David had always taken his elder brother duties very seriously so he stuck it out, keeping his younger brother desultory company as Harry admired the herd of elephants and the pride of lions – marvels of modern taxidermy.

It was only when Harry noticed David had gone white and there was a sickly film of sweat on his forehead that he realised he needed to get his brother back to Brooklyn. By the time they got home, David was feeling dizzy and having trouble standing up. Harry was beginning to feel sick too, but he didn't mention it. He was feeling bad about the way he had behaved.

The Friedmans had taken their elder son to the Beth-El Hospital and when they got back Harry was delirious with a fever. He was taken in too. Harry and his brother were among the first casualties of the 1941 polio epidemic.

No one really understood how it was transmitted. Was it touch, was it airborne in the breath or a sneeze, or was it something unknown? The hot weather seemed to stir it up and every few years the summer months would be blighted by an awful dread as the disease scythed through the children and teenagers of the area.

Its effects were completely unpredictable too. The great strapping athlete who played in the school football team would die in a couple of days; the delicate boy who was always ill would shrug it off with barely a scar. Sometimes polio left you with withered legs that could no longer support your weight. Some were left paralysed, or brain damaged. Sometimes you had to spend the rest of your life in an iron lung, when the disease stopped the muscles that made you breathe from working.

Harry had been one of those polio victims who'd been unmarked by the disease once it had worked its way through him. David had died. Harry had never told his parents he'd persuaded his brother to stay at the museum. And ever since he'd wondered whether they could have saved David if he'd got to hospital a few hours earlier.

That was the thing that made him volunteer for the air force. It was to make amends for that. If God wanted to punish him, then He would have a perfect opportunity.

That afternoon a fresh breeze blew in from the North Sea and the sun came out. Harry walked to the airbase perimeter and stared through the wire fence over a late crop of golden barley. He wanted to reach out and touch it as it rolled and rippled in the wind. He loved the way you could see the wind when you were watching a field of crops or wild grass. The chimes of Saint Mary's, the local village church, drifted over the field and he was seized by a painful awareness of the passing of time and his own little place in the world. Soon the crew of the *Macey May* would find their names on the combat roster. Who knew what would happen then?

CHAPTER 5

September 12th, 1943

That evening, as they assembled for a final inspection on the concrete in front of their B-17, Holberg outlined their flight plan.

'We're flying north-west to Birmingham, then over the Pennines and up to Edinburgh, then we have a long trail back over the North Sea. We'll be making our way up to a final height of twenty-five thousand feet so you'll be on oxygen. We'll stay up there until the final hour, when we'll descend to nine thousand and you'll be able to breathe without your masks. We should be home about 2.30 a.m.'

The *Macey May* took off just as the first hint of dusk began to colour the edge of the sky. Ten minutes into the flight, Harry squeezed into his ball turret, from where he had a wonderful view of an English autumn evening. Flying over a network of waterways in Norfolk he saw a painted canal boat making its leisurely passage east, a thin stream of white smoke trailing behind it. Harry considered for a moment whether he'd rather swap places with the boatman. No, he decided boldly. For all the dangers he faced, who could imagine seeing the things he was seeing?

There on the underside of the ascending B-17 he felt invincible. As they headed north, the shadows crept across the fields and he peered in wonder until they were too high to distinguish such detail on the ground. Holberg's voice came over the interphone: 'Beautiful, isn't it? But don't get distracted, you gunners. There's always the chance the Krauts will have some random patrols up here.'

By now night was almost upon them. After it got dark, if there were Nazi night fighters to contend with, they would not know they were there until the *Macey May* shook with the impact of cannon shells.

After half an hour they flew over a great urban conglomeration, just visible through the gloom. The city was observing the blackout well enough, and when it got properly dark it would be almost invisible from a height. 'We're just flying over Birmingham,' a voice came through his headphones. It was Warren Cain, the navigator. He had a busy night ahead of him, trying to maintain a sense of where they were, with nothing more than the stars, dead reckoning and radio-positioning signals to help him.

A great flash of light burst then faded below. 'Bomb explosion on the ground, three o' clock,' said Harry.

Stearley replied. 'Birmingham's a big industrial town – lots of iron and steel down there – just like Birmingham in Alabama. That'll be a blast furnace, not a bomb.'

Sure enough, there were several more bright bursts of light on the ground, as they headed over the great industrial belt to the north of Birmingham. Then they were out above open countryside again and there was nothing to be seen at all.

After an hour's flying Harry was getting cold and stiff in his cramped little perch in spite of his heated suit. He pressed his communication button and asked Holberg if he could come back into the aircraft for a brief period.

'No,' came the terse reply. 'Wait until it gets properly dark. I want you gunners on full alert. We all heard what happened to those guys over Molesworth.'

A few days ago, a flight of B-24 Liberators had been coming back from a raid at dusk when they were pounced by German night fighters. They had their landing lights on, and the runway lights were also switched on. It had been a massacre.

Twenty minutes later, Holberg's voice came over the interphone. 'OK, Friedman, you can come out for a few minutes. Go help Lieutenant Cain. See if you can get a position with the sextant.'

Harry squeezed out and made his unsteady way past the radio operator's compartment, the bomb bay catwalk, the pilots' cabin and finally to the bombardier and navigator's station, with its great Plexiglas nose cone, at the front of the plane.

Holberg was keen for his crew to widen their experience and had encouraged Harry to try his hand at navigation after Harry had told him he was a straight A math student. Harry realised that Holberg had asked him because he wanted his men to be able to do anything on the plane in case there was an emergency. If Cain was killed in their forward position, Holberg would need another navigator to plot a route home.

Harry had quickly got the hang of it. Plotting your position by the stars was something mariners had been doing since the dawn of history. And here they were now in the most technologically advanced aircraft, practising those same techniques – sextant pointing to the stars, getting their bearings in a manner invented by the ancient Greeks.

Holberg squeezed down into the nose.

'We should be over Edinburgh in about an hour,' Cain told the captain when he noticed he was standing behind them.

Holberg put a hand on Harry's shoulder. 'Back to your turret now, Sergeant. You're going to have to get used to long stretches in there. When we're over enemy territory, we'll have to be combat-ready for hours.'

Harry knew Holberg was right. Their final training would be over in a matter of days. They could be in combat by the end of the week. Then he would be living a life where you could not expect to survive from one day to the next.

The rest of the flight to Scotland was uneventful and they arrived over Edinburgh just after midnight. Harry could see the whole of a great estuary by the city illuminated in the moonlight. 'Firth of Forth down below,' said Cain over the interphone.

Once past the Firth, the B-17 began to bank as it took a leisurely turn through 180 degrees towards the south. Harry peered through the gloom to the dark city below. A big rock loomed large in the middle and he could see elegant curving streets and squares.

Cain's voice came over the interphone with navigation instructions. 'South by south-east . . .' This was the course intended to take them over the sea. He sounded utterly relaxed. Cain had been a surveyor before he joined the Eighth Air Force and Harry found it difficult to imagine him doing such a dry job. He was a friendly guy and he never pulled rank on the non-coms. Harry was struck by how much he liked him.

Once over the water, the weather abruptly changed and the ride got bumpier.

'We're just catching the end of a storm front here,' announced Holberg over the interphone.

Skaggs came over. 'Weather report says it's heading north, so we shouldn't have to put up with this turbulence much longer.'

Harry had flown enough to not mind a bit of turbulence. When he'd first been up in a B-17, the shaking and rattling during a bad storm had frightened the pants off him. He kept thinking the wings would fall off or the plane would break up in mid-air. Holberg had told them the Fortress was immensely sturdy and he was even sure he could even fly the thing upside down if he had to.

Skaggs's radio report on the weather had been wrong. The storm they flew through did not let up and the aircraft continued to shake and jolt violently. This was the worst storm any of them had been in. The next hour was marked by increasingly tense exchanges over the interphone between Holberg, Stearley and Cain.

A dull thud shook the fuselage as a bright flash passed through the aircraft.

'We've been hit,' called Skaggs over the interphone.

'Krauts can't be out in this?' screamed John in disbelief.

Holberg cut in. 'Anyone see anything?'

There was silence.

'OK, report.'

The crew called out their names, working from nose to tail. Harry listened intently. They were all there. No one had been hit.

'Well, that's something,' said Holberg. 'I think we were struck by lightning.' There was a pause, then Harry heard him say, 'Hey, look at that, Lieutenant. The directional giro has gone haywire.'

Then he said, 'We're going to climb to rise above this turbulence. Cain, I think we need another fix on our position. Check it out as soon as we break through the clouds.'

Harry thought Cain would be hurt that Holberg was clearly questioning his directions. But his instant response on the interphone sounded like he was in a really good mood.

'Wilco, Captain. Those stars are sure gonna look pretty after all this.'

Harry, isolated from the crew in his turret, was startled by loud crashes above him. 'It's OK, guys,' said Skaggs. 'Nothing to worry about. That was just a bit of stored equipment falling out of its locker.'

Holberg cut in. 'We'll be up at twenty-five thousand feet in the next ten minutes, and that should give us a smoother flight.'

When they did level out, the engines stopped screaming and clawing for height and settled into their deep familiar drone. The whole sky below was covered in cloud. It looked beautiful in the moonlight – like a fluffy white sea. Occasionally lightning would spark beneath the clouds, giving them an eerie glow.

The next ten minutes passed in silence until Harry realised he had accidentally unplugged his headphone socket. When he patched it back in he was alarmed to hear Cain giving increasingly confusing directions to Holberg.

The captain was unable to hide his impatience. 'Warren, take another reading from the astrodome for God's sake. See if you can establish a more accurate position.'

A few minutes later, Cain's voice crackled in Harry's ears again. 'Current estimate: landfall over Scarborough approximately twenty minutes.'

'OK, Lieutenant Cain,' said Holberg, trying to sound calm and casual. 'Attention, *Macey May*,' he continued, 'it's looking calmer down there so we'll take her down to five thousand feet and check our bearings.'

As they began their slow descent, Harry's ears popped until he swallowed. Soon the glowing cloud tops were just below them. It seemed magical to him, slung beneath the B-17, to suddenly start skimming the clouds' surface but not feel a thing. If he could have stuck his feet over the side of his turret, he could have dipped them in, like a sailor in a little boat, trailing his feet in a river.

Now the *Macey May* was enveloped in cloud and darkness was complete. It was very unsettling, not being able to see a thing all around. A few minutes later they were out the other side and Holberg was on the interphone again. 'Hey, Friedman, any landmarks, towns or cities, church steeples, rivers? We should definitely be over the east coast by now.'

'It's a complete blank, Captain,' said Harry. 'Cloud must be blocking all moonlight. Blackout below is total.'

'We'll take her further down. Friedman, keep your eyes on the ground – shout if you see any hills, trees, whatever.'

They descended some more. Holberg kept asking, every few minutes. He was obviously getting concerned. 'Friedman, you awake down there? We're at one thousand feet now, going down to five hundred. Shout the second you see anything.'

Harry felt indignant. He was straining to see anything at all in the darkness. He was feeling especially vulnerable in his ball turret and wanted to ask Holberg if he could get back in the plane. If they hit the ground, he would be the first to know about it – in the split second before he was mangled to death. But no one could see the ground better than him, and he knew Holberg would order him to remain at his station.

Harry continued to slowly rotate his turret 360 degrees around its axis, tilting it almost 90 degrees so he could look straight down. It was tiring hanging from his straps as gravity pulled on him. Then he levelled the turret to take in the wider horizon. Perhaps ten miles to the east, Harry spotted a shaft of moonlight.

'Captain, think I can see waves down there,' he reported.

'Well, North Sea's supposed to be over to the east,' said Holberg, 'so that's telling us something useful. Keep looking, Sergeant.'

Jim Corrales chipped in. 'Smells like the sea, here at the tail. I'd guess we were still over the water.'

'I'll take us down another couple hundred feet,' said Holberg.

A minute later, another shaft of moonlight broke through and Harry saw at once the white caps of breaking waves. In an instant the Fortress flew over a small fishing boat, close enough for Harry to see the startled faces of the men on board. 'Captain, we're right down over the sea. Pull up, pull up,' he shouted.

Holberg didn't comply. Harry heard him say, 'Landing lights on, Lieutenant Stearley.'

Intense white beams pierced the gloom and, sure enough, they revealed a choppy sea almost close enough to touch.

Harry couldn't stop himself from yelling out, 'It's the sea! We're about to hit the frigging sea.'

'Hold tight,' said the captain. The engines screamed as they climbed a thousand feet. 'Cain, I think we have to admit we're lost.'

There was no reply. Holberg continued, 'Skaggs, I want you to start transmitting a Mayday signal. We need to get a position here.'

Harry felt a twist of fear. Lone transmissions at this time of night over the North Sea were bound to attract the attention of the Luftwaffe. Those signals enabled their tracking stations to pinpoint the position of a bomber. Depending on where they were, they might have a Nazi night fighter on their tail within minutes.

Skaggs came on the interphone a few minutes later. 'We've had a fix from Attlebridge. We're 53°40' North, 5°34' East.'

'Can you plot a route back for us on that, Lieutenant Cain?' Holberg sounded unsure. Harry could tell he had lost faith in his navigator.

'Wilco,' came Cain's terse response.

Harry continued his 360-degree survey of the sky. The cloud cover was breaking up, and luminous shafts of moonlight were lighting up patches of the sea. 'Captain, there's a string of islands about ten miles to the east,' he shouted.

'I see them too,' said John.

'Shit,' said Stearley. 'Those have got to be the Wadden Islands. There's a whole chain of them off the Dutch coast.'

'OK, here's what we're going to do,' said Holberg. He sounded terse, but his voice was steady. 'LaFitte, I need a fuel supply estimate as quickly as you can. Work out how long it'll take to reach the English coast and what our optimum cruising speed should be to preserve fuel. The rest of you, watch out for night fighters. Skaggs, keep radio silence until absolutely necessary.'

Harry knew what that meant. If they were going to crash, then Skaggs would be at his post until the last few seconds, transmitting a distress signal.

Five minutes later, Holberg came over the interphone again. 'OK. We're heading straight for the British coast, but for now we're in enemy airspace. Keep looking for fighters.'

The next thirty minutes passed in an anxious silence. Then Dalinsky called out to report the exhaust plume of a Nazi fighter at three o' clock level. Harry tensed up, expecting the *Macey May* to be raked with cannon fire at any moment.

There was a rattle of machine-gun fire and at once the interphone sprang into life, with Hill, Dalinsky and Corrales all shouting excitedly.

'Fellas, pipe down,' said Holberg. 'Was that them or us?'

'I fired off a few rounds, Captain,' said Dalinsky. 'Thought I saw a shape over to the right.'

Holberg was admirably calm. 'Everyone take a good look and report back immediately if you can see any aircraft around us.'

There was another minute's silence, then the interphone came to life with all the gunners reporting they could see nothing in the black sky. Five minutes passed, then ten. If there had been a night fighter, it had lost them.

Harry kept rotating his turret, looking out for any sign of a coastal outline but all he could see was the sea. Fifteen minutes later LaFitte came over the interphone. 'We've only got fuel for another fifteen minutes, Captain.'

'OK, *Macey May*, I want you to prepare to ditch,' Holberg said. 'I don't think we'll make it to land.'

There was an ominous pause, then he said, 'Skaggs, transmit our position as soon as Cain can give it you . . . And try to get a position for the nearest airfield along the coast. We should be close to the Wash by now, so we might get lucky.' Then he added, 'Sergeant Friedman, you can come out of the ball now.'

As others in the crew carried out last-minute checks, Holberg told any crew who were not occupied to throw anything they could out of the Fortress. It was just like being on a ship that was in danger of sinking. Even the guns had to go – out through the open bomb bay doors.

Harry passed his own machine guns up to John Hill through the open ball turret hatch. It was a relief to be out of that little steel ball, but he could die just as easily in the plane with the rest of them. Despite his fear he felt a fleeting regret that this magnificent machine, with its thousands of carefully assembled and maintained working parts, would shortly become a rusting heap of junk at the bottom of the sea.

His duty done, he went to join the others who had congregated in the radio operator's compartment between the bomb bay and his turret. Only Holberg and Stearley were left in the front of their aircraft. Harry didn't envy them, with the awful responsibility of a night ditching. No one in their right mind would want to put a B-17 down in a choppy sea.

If Holberg screwed up the landing and dipped the tail in first, rather than landing level, then the most likely place for the B-17 to break in two was the exact spot they were all sitting. He tried not to think of what would happen to them if that occurred. They'd be flying at 100 miles an hour. They'd be killed for sure.

'Life vests on,' said Bortz, the bombardier, who was the most senior officer there among them. 'And don't go inflating them before we're out the plane.'

They all placed their yellow life vests over their heads and they checked one another's to make sure they had fastened the harnesses correctly. Skaggs stayed at his post transmitting a steady stream of Mayday messages. Harry wondered if anyone was responding. Skaggs seemed to be transmitting into a void.

Cain was fidgeting and would not catch anyone's eye. No one spoke to him either, although John still checked his life vest's harness. Clearly the crew was blaming him for their situation.

Over the deep drone of the engines, Harry heard Skaggs's voice catch. 'Hallelujah!' he said. 'Read you . . . *Macey May*, call sign G-20, Heavy Bombardment Group 488, Eighth Air Force, based at Kirkstead. Current location approximately twenty miles east of Norfolk coast, just about level with Cromer and heading towards the Wash. We're ditching and require immediate assistance . . .'

The engine note changed dramatically. LaFitte, the engineer, immediately called over to Skaggs. 'Captain's cut the two inboard, contact imminent.'

Skaggs did not need to be asked twice. He immediately joined the others crouching against the bulkheads, wrapping the cushion on his seat around his head. The compartment doorway flew open and Harry looked through it at the central spar which held his ball turret in place and wondered what would happen to it when it hit the water. Thank God he wasn't stuck inside it. Corrales quickly shut the door again.

'That'll make a big difference,' he said with a nervous grin.

Only Bortz was plugged into the interphone system, but he was getting nothing from the pilot's cabin. 'I'm going to check they're all right.'

Cain looked up from his crash position. 'Let me go. It's too dangerous. We're gonna hit the water any second. I got us into this mess . . .'

Just as he got to his feet the engines screamed as the *Macey May* lifted a little in the air. Bortz shouted, 'Brace!'

and there was a huge jolt. Cain crouched down again, just in time.

Another jolt followed, perhaps the crest of a wave, then the overwhelming drone of the engines ceased. There was a sudden massive deceleration and they were all thrown against the bulkhead. Another sickening lurch twisted them back and forth as the plane pitched to the right. A nightmarish screeching sound from beyond the closed door filled the radio compartment and Harry thought the belly of the plane might open up beneath them. He sensed they were still travelling at some speed and prayed that the *Macey May* would hold together.

CHAPTER 6

Harry's pants were soaked. For one awful moment he wondered if he'd wet himself but the smell of salty sea water filled his nostrils and he quickly realised there were now sloshing pools of water along the floor of the *Macey May*. He felt a mad panic and an overwhelming urge to escape.

The engines were silent and they sensed the plane had stopped moving forward in the water. Now it just rocked with the waves. The sound of the sea was all around them, even the cawing of a few startled gulls.

Bortz was looking grim but composed. In fact they all were. Harry was struck by how calmly his comrades had behaved. He was desperate to know what lay beyond that compartment door to the rear of the plane, and whether they would be able to get out of the exit there before the Fortress sank. He tried hard to keep his fear under control and not give them any reason to think he was a flaky kid who had lied about his age to get into the USAAF.

Dalinsky was the first on his feet and pulled the life raft handles, releasing them from their two stowage boxes at the side of the outer fuselage. They would inflate automatically as soon as they hit the water.

A wave broke against the side of the *Macey May*, making the Fortress tilt alarmingly to the right. 'Let's go,' said Bortz. Out they went, through the compartment door, Corrales first, then the two waist gunners, then Harry, then the rest – just like they did in the drill. Harry noticed at once that the ball turret had been torn from its housing, leaving a livid scar of ripped metal along the belly. Water surged through, rising and falling with the swell. The limitless depth of the sea beneath the ruptured aluminium frame filled him with foreboding.

'Exit door's jammed!' Corrales shouted back to them. Dalinsky, right behind him, gave it an almighty kick and it sprang open with a grinding of bent metal. Water poured in as the aircraft dipped in the waves. Harry felt the icy blast of the sea, but nothing was going to stop him leaving the aircraft.

He plunged into the freezing water and was immediately submerged. His heavy flying suit dragged him down into pitch-black water, where he didn't know which way was up. *Pull your cord*, a voice inside his head said. He fumbled for the cord with clumsy gloves and the life vest filled with compressed air. At once he found himself rising to the surface like a cork, but almost immediately his head hit something hard. He was still underwater and realised he was trapped somewhere under the plane. In his panic he couldn't find his way free but then felt someone tugging him by the arm.

Now he was above the surface, drawing in gasping lungfuls of air.

John was there by his side, holding on to his arm. 'Harry's out,' he shouted.

Harry realised now that he had come up under the wing. Dalinsky was already up on it, swaying unsteadily in the swell of the sea. Corrales was crouching on the edge, holding the tethers of both the life rafts.

Dalinsky dragged Harry and John out of the sea. So far the B-17 was still level. 'Who else is out there?' said Corrales. Cain dragged himself up the wing, and then Skaggs, LaFitte and Bortz followed.

'Well, that's most of us,' said Bortz. 'Where're Holberg and Stearley?'

Dark though it was, there was still enough moonlight to see the pilot's cabin. The right window was closed – a bad sign. That was one of the pilots' emergency exits. Cain dived into the sea and reached the rear exit in a few quick strokes. Bortz shouted, 'Come back, Warren. She could go under at any second.'

The water level was already up to the door.

Cain levered himself up and peered into the dark interior.

Harry said, 'I'm going to help him,' but Bortz held him back.

'Friedman, you stay here. This plane is going under any second. There's no point wasting both your lives.'

Even as he said it, the Fortress's nose dipped down lower

in the swell – enough for the rear exit to nearly clear the surface of the sea. They all felt the wing tilt, but then the Fortress seemed to steady itself. Harry knew he couldn't just stand and watch. Bortz had let go his arm, and without another word he dived back into the water. When he reached the hatch, he pulled himself up, his waterlogged clothes hanging heavy on his body.

Peering down into the darkened interior, he realised his task was hopeless. What happened next startled him. The lights inside the plane came on.

Wading through the waterlogged interior, Harry reached the cabin to find Cain and Holberg wrenching at Stearley's harnesses. The co-pilot had passed out and was trapped in his seat. 'Warren, get me the toolkit. Just by your table.'

Cain wrenched off his bulky life jacket and threw it to Harry, then squeezed through the narrow passageway beneath the pilots' seats. As he opened the small wooden door Harry saw freezing cold water gush around his legs. There must be at least a foot of it swilling round in there. They all felt the B-17 dip lower in the water as Cain's weight shifted the centre of gravity. Within seconds he had found the tool case and quickly returned to the cabin.

'What do you need?' he asked.

'Hacksaw.'

Cain handed it over and Holberg began to desperately saw at the tough canvas strap. Stearley started to moan and then struggle. 'Hold still, Curtis,' said Cain, putting a reassuring hand on his shoulder. 'We'll get you out in just a second.'

'You deadbeat,' said Stearley, with sudden wide-eyed aggression. 'You got us into this frigging mess.'

Holberg pushed him down in his seat. 'Not now, Curtis,' he said angrily. 'We need to get you out of here. This man is trying to save your life.'

Harry passed Cain his life jacket. 'You'd better put this back on, Lieutenant.'

Cain gave him a grim smile. 'Thank you for coming to help,' he said.

It took another twenty seconds of frantic sawing to cut through the harness.

'Do you think you can walk?'

Stearley nodded.

'Let's go,' said Holberg. But Stearley was still too unsteady on his feet and quickly collapsed in the swirling sea water.

'We need to get him out by that rear exit,' said Cain. 'He'll never make it out through a window.'

Holberg, Cain and Harry grabbed Stearley and struggled to drag him through the cramped interior.

'Let me be,' said the co-pilot. 'I can walk.'

The *Macey May* lurched forward and they almost lost their balance.

'Quick,' said Holberg. 'She's about to go down.'

The interior was constructed of a series of alloy rings, and the three of them grabbed hold of them to steady themselves as they dragged Stearley towards the rear, Cain and Holberg pulling on his arms, Harry behind, holding his feet. As they reached the rear exit the plane lifted right out of the water by about twenty degrees and Harry lost his footing, sliding down towards the mangled wreckage of the waist.

He hit his head when he stopped and felt momentarily dazed, then saw Cain making his way back to help him. 'Come on, Friedman, we've got to get out of here fast.'

They looked up to see Holberg standing at the exit, pulling the compressed air handle on Stearley's life jacket and pushing him out back first, then Holberg shouted over to the men on the wing, 'Into the rafts, boys. Get away from her before she goes down.'

He hesitated at the door, looking down the fuselage at Harry and Cain, struggling to regain their footing. 'Come on, men, get back up here,' he shouted. 'Don't get sucked under.'

'Captain, jump,' they heard Corrales shout from outside.

The Fortress shifted again as the nose filled with water. Holberg started to climb down the interior, but the closer he got the more the plane dipped down. With a supreme effort Harry and Cain managed to claw their way back up to the exit, now fighting gravity as well as their waterlogged flight suits.

'Come on!' urged Holberg.

But he waited, knowing his weight was keeping the Fortress from dipping further, and when Harry and then Cain came within reach he held out a hand to help them.

Holberg pushed Harry out and he landed face first in the sea, the shock of the freezing water taking his breath away. There was another splash right next to him. It was Cain. They surfaced to see Holberg still framed by the doorway.

They watched the bedraggled figure of the captain hesitate at the doorway. Then he jumped too.

Stearley was still floating in the water, too weak and dazed to help himself. Seeing him a few feet away, Harry dragged the co-pilot back to the nearest raft, which Corrales, John Hill and Dalinsky had now occupied. It took the three of them, and several near capsizes, to drag the co-pilot and Harry into the raft.

The tail end of the Fortress was now forty degrees up from the water. The nose had disappeared and water washed around the pilots' cabin. They could still see the eerie glow of the internal lights just below the surface.

The B-17 swung further to the upright, its massive tail section hanging over them all. There it stood for a few moments as Holberg and Cain swam frantically towards the other life raft.

The *Macey May* gave another lurch then slowly began to sink into the sea. Now the wings were gone entirely and trapped air continued to belch and hiss from within. The tail hung suspended for a few more seconds, then a great bubble of air surfaced around it and it vanished into the depths.

LaFitte, Bortz and Skaggs had boarded the other life raft and they dragged Holberg and Cain in with them. As the two rafts bumped against each other Holberg said, 'Tie 'em together, quick.' He looked utterly exhausted, but he continued with the drill.

'Emergency compass?' asked Holberg. 'Spare radio? Pigeon?'

The rest of the crew looked blank. In their blind panic to escape, they had forgotten almost everything they had been trained to salvage.

Harry expected an excoriating dressing-down from the captain, but Holberg didn't have the energy or the heart.

'OK,' he said plainly. 'We're freezing to death, we don't know where we are, and there's nothing we can do to call for help. Any suggestions?'

Harry glanced at Corrales, praying there was no smartass quip on his lips. The tail gunner held up a paddle. 'At least we got one of these, Captain.'

Harry had barely noticed the cold, apart from the initial paralysing shock when he entered the sea. But now he realised he was desperately, dangerously cold – colder than he could ever have imagined.

'We gotta huddle together, try to keep warm,' said Dalinsky.

'You've been reading your survival guide,' said Holberg. 'Well done, Sergeant.'

LaFitte surprised them all. 'I got a thermos with me. Let's hope it hasn't cracked.'

'LaFitte, you're a hero,' said Holberg wearily. 'Stearley first, then let's all take a sip.'

They all took a mouthful of hot milky coffee, except Cain, who waved the thermos away.

Holberg insisted. 'Cain, you just saved Stearley's life.'

The men usually joked that the coffee in the canteen was 'battery acid', but at that moment Harry thought it was the most delicious thing he'd ever tasted in his life. Even a small amount helped clear away the salty taste of the sea from his throat, and warmed him slightly. But seconds later they were all shivering uncontrollably, teeth chattering so much it was difficult to talk.

'We gotta paddle,' said Hill. 'Keep warm.'

'I know,' said Holberg. 'But we've got to paddle in the right direction. 'We don't want to be halfway back to Holland by the time the sun comes up.'

Harry knew they could be half dead of exposure by then.

'OK, we've got to keep the blood flowing,' said Holberg. He got them to all rub each other's arms and backs. It took their minds off how cold they actually were.

'Now let's frighten the fish with a sing-song,' he said. 'What do we all know?'

They sang a mad version of Glen Miller's 'In the Mood', each of them pretending to play the saxophones, trumpets and trombones of that ever-popular instrumental number.

Harry started to laugh. It was bizarre. Here they were, freezing to death but singing at the top of their voices. He looked at Bob Holberg with an overwhelming affection. What a great guy!

The moon came out from behind a cloud, and they could take a fix on where they were.

'The coast – look!' shouted Bortz. Harry couldn't believe his eyes. There were grey cliffs not half a mile away. They cheered themselves hoarse and all at once they began to frantically paddle towards land.

From that moment on, their luck changed. Cain spotted a branch floating in the sea and they grabbed that too as another makeshift oar. Within half an hour they felt the rafts hit gravelly seashore and they leaped out and found themselves on a deserted muddy beach.

Stearley had recovered enough to walk, and the bedraggled crew began to make their way inland.

As they reached the edge of the beach a shot flew over their heads. All ten of them threw themselves to the ground in an instant.

'What the hell's going on?' shouted Holberg. For one horrible moment Harry wondered if they had landed in occupied Europe after all.

'Sorry, lads,' came a sheepish voice. 'Thought we were being invaded.'

It was a squad of middle-aged and elderly men – a Home Guard detachment out on a night patrol. The Guard wasted no time looking after them. Within ten minutes they had been given hot drinks and dry clothes. By the time a truck had taken them back to Kirkstead it was still dark. The station had been alerted that they had been rescued, but when they arrived home no one greeted them except a few sleepy military policemen. They headed straight to their huts and collapsed in an exhausted stupor. Tomorrow they would have to face Colonel Kittering, who would, most definitely, be wanting an explanation.

CHAPTER 7

September 13th, 1943

In what remained of the night, Harry was tormented by a recurring dream. He was trapped in his ball turret. It felt like a goldfish bowl and it was filling up with sea water. Hitler, Goering, Goebbels and those other top Nazis he'd seen in the newsreels were outside laughing at him. He woke up in the morning spluttering and gasping for air, his body covered in cold sweat.

But at least he was still alive. Coming to his senses in the familiar confines of the hut, he realised the crew of the *Macey May* had had an extraordinarily lucky escape.

Holberg arrived at the hut at 10 a.m., anxious to get something off his chest, and John Hill and Harry woke the guys who were still asleep.

'You'll have plenty of time to rest over the next few days,' he explained as they sat in a weary semicircle around him. 'I think we'll all be sent on survival leave. But first there's going to be an investigation.'

'Will Cain be court-martialled, sir?' asked John.

'That's very much down to us,' said Holberg. 'The evidence is at the bottom of the North Sea, so they'll be going on what we tell them. I spoke to Cain before we went to sleep and he said he couldn't understand why he was so off beam with his coordinates. He did say he felt unusually light-headed and I think he may have been having problems with his oxygen. And that storm didn't help. That lightning strike definitely messed up the navigation instruments.'

He paused, looking awkward.

'I'll be straight with you. I know some of the other officers on *Macey May* want him thrown to the dogs. They think he should have known something was wrong and sorted it out.

'But I think we need to give him a second chance,' Holberg continued. 'He's as good a navigator as we're ever gonna get. He did a damn fine job on those training flights we did back home and he got us across the Atlantic . . .

'You guys screwed it up as well. We left the Fortress without our radio and other essential equipment. Apart from Dalinsky, who remembered to release the life rafts, we did virtually nothing right when we ditched.'

'Don't forget the paddle, chief,' Corrales said.

'That's unlikely to earn you a medal, Sergeant,' replied Holberg.

He paused again and looked round the group. 'I'm gonna leave you guys to talk things over. I hope you'll feel you can back Cain up, just like you'd want your buddies in the crew to back you up.' Then he left the hut.

The non-coms were divided over Cain.

'He could have killed us all,' said Dalinsky.

Corrales nodded. 'I don't wanna fly a long mission with someone who's gonna screw up. We got enough to worry about with the flak and the fighters.'

'It wasn't all down to Cain – you can't blame him for that storm blowing up,' Skaggs said.

'Cain knows his stuff,' Harry said. 'He was acting kinda strange. We shoulda realised he wasn't getting enough oxygen. I think we should give him another chance.'

Corrales and Dalinsky still looked uncertain.

John spoke next. 'I like Cain. He doesn't hold himself above the rest of us like some of the officers. I'm for giving him another chance.'

Harry chipped in again. 'We're a good team. We've been training together for five months now. I don't want to go into combat with a stranger. It wouldn't be the same.'

'Yeah, there is that. We could get someone even worse,' said Corrales.

'How about it, fellas? Are we gonna back Cain up?' Harry asked.

John Hill and Clifford Skaggs nodded, then Corrales.

'I guess so,' said Dalinsky finally.

Harry's face lit up. 'I'll go tell the captain.'

Soon after midday Harry and his hut mates were disturbed again. This time it was Bortz. 'Shift yourselves, boys,' he called through the door. 'We've all got to report to the MO.'

They sat together in the base hospital, in a stark waiting area, all feeling deflated, almost despondent. On their way there they passed the intensive-care section. They'd all glimpsed the guy in there, wrapped head to toe in bandages and plaster. John whispered he must be a burns victim or something. Or maybe he had burns and a lot of broken bones. 'Even if he survives he's going to be a real mess,' he said. It was a fate none of them wanted to think about – utterly helpless, surrounded by doctors and nurses talking in concerned, hushed voices.

The co-pilot was missing. 'Is Lieutenant Stearley all right?' Harry asked.

'He's on a ward. Twenty-four-hour observation,' said Holberg. 'That was a nasty bump he got when we landed. Concussion. I'm sure he's going to be OK though.'

The station medical officer, a gruff civilian doctor who had come out of retirement to serve with the air force, checked each of the crew over – the usual battery of tests for reflexes, heart rate, pulse . . .

Harry's turn came to enter the examination cubicle.

'Any aches, pains you've noticed? Anything unusual?'

'I slept pretty bad, sir, last night,' said Harry, and he mentioned his dream.

The doctor took out a brown glass jar and shook out a little black pill. 'That'll sort you out, son,' he said. 'Take it just before you turn in for the night. You're lucky not to be suffering from exposure after a midnight ditching in the North Sea.'

In a few minutes, the doctor had declared him fit for active service and Harry rejoined the others back in the waiting room.

'Ditching should be worth at least twenty-four hours on the observation ward,' Corrales grumbled.

'There's a war on, Sergeant,' Bortz said wearily.

Harry was surprised to find himself agreeing with Bortz. Putting them on the ward would have been unnecessary mollycoddling. He was proud of the way his crew had got through their ordeal. They were tougher than he had realised.

But he hoped this didn't mean he would lose that survival leave Holberg had mentioned. John Hill had asked if he would like to go to Edinburgh with him and he didn't want to miss out on that.

As they waited for the all-clear from the MO they hunched together to speak in low voices.

'I've got to see Kittering this afternoon,' said Holberg. 'I know what he's going to say to me.'

Corrales mimicked the colonel's gritty voice. 'Uncle Sam pays quarter of a million dollars each for a B-17 . . .'

Holberg silenced him with a stern look.

'I wanted to talk to you all together, and this seems like the best opportunity. If they grill us all in debriefing, we've got to have the same story. Cain, you flew us over the Atlantic, you flew us all that way from Nebraska, for Chrissakes; you've always been spot on. Tell us all again what happened last night.'

'I still don't really know how I got it so wrong.' Cain looked desperate. 'Like I said, I wasn't feeling myself on that flight. I was fine to begin with, but a few hours in I started to feel light-headed. I don't know if it was the cold, but I just felt really detached from everything . . .'

LaFitte spoke up, barely able to contain his hostility. 'Lieutenant, didn't you recognise anoxia symptoms from your training?'

'I guess I should have realised, but I was having a hell of a job trying to keep our bearings in that storm and I suppose I just didn't think about it.'

'Sounds like a faulty oxygen mask to me.' Holberg put a sympathetic hand on his shoulder. 'Lieutenant, in other circumstances I'd be recommending you for a Congressional Medal of Honor. Lieutenant Stearley and I would both have gone down with the *Macey May* if you and Friedman hadn't come to rescue us.'

He turned his gaze to the rest of the crew.

'Well, we all screwed up in our separate ways. Even Stearley and I. We were so caught up in landing the Fortress level we didn't even tell you when we were about to make contact.'

'Hey, chief,' said Skaggs. 'You saved our lives. I heard B-17s can disintegrate if you don't get that landing right.'

'Well, I'll level with you. I don't want any of this to get back to Kittering. If the colonel finds out how bad we messed up, we'll all be on the next transport back to the States. So are you with me?'

They all nodded, even LaFitte, although he was looking pretty sour about it. Harry suspected some of them might relish the opportunity to get out of this, but no one said anything.

At that moment, the MO came into the waiting area. 'You can all go back to your huts and rest for the day. You've had a lucky escape.'

Holberg called them together again, outside the hospital entrance, and spoke quietly. 'OK. Good. I'll have a word with Lieutenant Stearley when I go and visit him. As far as I'm concerned, we blame this on exceptionally rough weather and faulty equipment. That, and the lightning strike. Assuming they buy it, and assuming they keep us here, I want you all to read up on oxygen failure and how that makes you feel. And as soon as we're back on duty we'll be running those ditching drills until we can do them blindfolded.'

CHAPTER 8

Kittering was due to see Holberg at three that afternoon. He wasn't looking forward to the encounter. He liked Holberg. He had a fresh-faced openness, almost an innocence, and the idea of sending a man like that to face almost certain death gnawed at the colonel in the dead of the night. He'd been a junior pilot himself, back in the first war, flying with the American Air Service over Flanders.

That had been a fiasco right from the start. For every pilot killed in combat, two were killed in training. And the ones who lived long enough to fly in an operational squadron rarely lasted more than a month. The only thing that held them together, that kept them flying, was that they were more frightened of their commanding officer than they were of death itself.

Kittering modelled himself on that man – Colonel Carl Bufford. The airmen had hated him at the time, and everyone on the base called him 'Iron Ass'. But afterwards, when it was over, and Kittering was the only one of his intake to survive, he began to think Bufford was just the kind of man you needed to lead a bomb group in wartime.

The planes were safer now, but combat was just as dangerous. In the First War Bufford had flown with his men, shared their danger, and that was something that had really impressed Kittering. He would have liked to do the same now, but the Eighth Air Force commander-in-chief, General Eaker, had expressly forbidden him to do so. Some bull about being too valuable to lose. He should have felt flattered, but he thought it made him look like a coward to the men.

Kittering decided he was going to have to give Holberg a roasting. He might like him, but he seriously doubted he had the mettle to command a B-17.

There was a knock at the door.

'Come the hell in,' he bellowed.

Holberg put his head round the door. He looked unsure of himself, almost sheepish.

'I hear things are a bit slack on the *Macey May*, Captain,' said Kittering. 'How else can I account for the loss of a quarter-million-dollar airplane on a training exercise?'

'My crew did their best in difficult circumstances, sir,' said Holberg. 'We lost out way in a storm on our return from Edinburgh. Our Fortress was also hit by lightning, which affected our navigational instruments. And I have very strong reasons for suspecting Lieutenant Cain had a faulty oxygen supply.'

The colonel listened in stony silence.

Holberg felt compelled to continue. 'Cain has performed extremely well until now. In training he brought us over the States, and then over the Atlantic to Kirkstead, with no trouble at all, and his ETA has always been right to the minute.'

Kittering cut in. 'Any damn fool navigator can estimate an aircraft time of arrival when all you have to worry about is getting a sunburn and what sort of chow you'll have to eat when you arrive there. You need a man who isn't going to crack under pressure. I'm going to take Cain off combat duty. If he wants to continue to fly, he's going to have to retrain as a gunner.'

'Colonel, I'm convinced there's some explanation for what happened. Cain showed exceptional courage after we had ditched, returning to the aircraft with Sergeant Friedman to rescue Lieutenant Stearley.'

Kittering liked the way Holberg was sticking up for his navigator. The man had nearly killed them all, yet his captain was trying to keep him. But Kittering's mind was made up. Bomber crews needed loyalty. That was how they got through the hell of combat operations. But a weak link would get them all killed.

'Cut the bullshit, Captain. Cain messed up. And even if it was his oxygen, he should have recognised the symptoms of anoxia. He's off this base by the end of the day. There's a Liberator flying back to New York this evening. I want him on that plane.'

Holberg opened his mouth to complain. Kittering butted in. 'Stow it. And I want to see your crew saluting you and addressing you as an officer. You'll thank me for it when you go into combat.'

82

Kittering was interrupted by a sharp knock at the door.

'Sorry to disturb you, sir,' said an orderly. 'Urgent message from High Wycombe.'

Holberg got up to go.

'Sit down,' Kittering snarled. 'We aren't done yet.'

The colonel scanned the message he'd been given from bomb group headquarters. It called for an immediate change of plan.

'Well, well,' he said, 'I changed my mind. I need twelve Fortresses combat-ready for imminent operations. Cain's on probation. You're all on the combat roster as of now.'

'But, sir, we were told we were due survival leave,' blurted Holberg.

'Cancelled,' said the colonel. 'Dismissed!'

Harry was reading a month-old copy of *Time* magazine when Holberg came over to the hut later that afternoon. They all looked up from their beds and chairs. Harry could tell Holberg was milking the moment, trying to look inscrutable. But he couldn't keep the smile from his face. 'We're off the hook!' he announced with a grin.

The non-coms looked at him quizzically. Then they noticed Stearley was right behind him.

'Lieutenant!' asked Dalinsky. 'What's the story?'

Stearley gave them all a winning smile. 'Doc says I'm OK. Another day and I'm A1 fit.'

Holberg continued with his news. 'Kittering's assigning us a new aircraft and we're all staying together.'

They gave a cheer.

'He also told me we're now on combat duty. So congratulations, guys. We passed the audition!'

Their faces fell.

'What about our survival leave?' asked Dalinsky.

Holberg put on a brave face. 'I'm sorry, boys – that's been cancelled. We've got a war to fight.'

The men let out a collective moan of disappointment.

He turned to John Hill. 'Sergeant Hill, you did a great job with the nose art on our previous Fortress. Can you paint *Macey May II* on the side of our new airplane as soon as you're able? Lieutenant Stearley can help you if he feels up to it. We can worry about a picture later, but nothing too racy this time, if you don't mind.'

Holberg had them walk over to see their new aircraft at the end of the day. Ernie Benik and his boys were already working on it, changing spark plugs and cleaning oil filters, balancing giros and clearing the static from the faulty interphone system. Holberg had been surprised how calmly his chief mechanic had taken the news that they had ditched *Macey May* in the North Sea.

Ernie told them it was his job to ensure none of the crew even thought they were flying a different plane. And if Holberg came back and told him the number-three engine was running warmer than usual, or the hydraulics still needed work, then he'd know exactly who to blame.

The *Macey May* boys had quickly realised how lucky they were to have Ernie Benik looking after them. The ground crew hut was close to the one Harry shared with his crew mates and the guys often popped in and out of each other's quarters when they were off duty. Ernie had hung a notice over the door of his hut: *The more trouble found on the ground, the less in the air.* And they knew he worked the ground crew day and night to make sure the *Macey May* was not going to let them down.

Ernie was especially good at getting spare parts, and he let the guys who didn't smoke know that their unused cigarette ration could be put to good use with local garages and supply depots, where he could get stuff quicker than the official air force channels.

It was getting dark by the time Holberg dismissed them. 'I don't know exactly when we're due to fly our first mission, but if you guys have letters to write, then get writing them sooner rather than later. And those of you who want to go to confession, or take Holy Communion – well, you all know where the pastor is.'

He was trying to be matter-of-fact about it, but they all knew the underlying reason.

Exhausted from the day's endeavours, Harry took his black pill and went early to bed. Despite the imminence of combat, he slept better. The vivid dreams did not return to haunt him; instead, he woke at first light with a nameless sense of dread. He asked Hill about the lack of dreams over breakfast.

'Little black pill?' John said. 'It's a placebo. Look it up.'

Harry went to the mess library and found a dictionary.

Placebo: *n. 1. a. A substance having no medication in its ingredients, given to a patient to reinforce their expectation to recover from their illness.*

The pill was a fake! He didn't know whether to feel angry or just laugh about his own gullibility.

CHAPTER 9

September 17th, 1943

'Wake up, Harry, big deal's going down today,' said Ernie Benik.

'What's happened?' said Harry, rubbing the sleep from his eyes. 'Have we got a mission today?'

'They'll tell you all about it at breakfast,' said Ernie. 'But don't worry. You ain't flying.'

Corrales filled Harry in over powdered eggs. 'Those lucky bastards in *Kansas Kate* have just finished their twenty-five missions. They came back yesterday from Friedrichshafen.'

Harry had noticed one bunch from a B-17 being carried aloft by their ground crew, but he'd assumed they'd had a lucky escape, or maybe shot down several Messerschmitts, or something like that. In truth he had been too preoccupied to enquire what all the fuss was about. He didn't like the airbase ritual of gathering by the control tower to count how many had made it back from a mission. It was too much of a taste of what was to come. The tension on the faces, the sinking feeling when you saw the flare being fired from an approaching Fortress to let the ground crews know there were injured men in need of urgent attention. All too soon the *Macey May* would be one of those returning Fortresses and who knew what was going to happen to them when they started operational flying.

Despite it all, the news from Corrales cheered him up. It gave them all a glimmer of hope. 'Ernie said there was something big happening,' said Harry.

'Only General Eaker flyin' in to give them a medal, and the King and Queen of England are coming too,' said Dalinsky.

Harry laughed out loud. Eaker was the Eighth Air Force commander-in-chief. He'd seen pictures of him in the air force newspaper, of course, but it would be interesting to see what he looked like in the flesh.

'What are the Limeys doing muscling in on this?' said Corrales. 'It's got nothing to do with them.'

John shook his head. 'Don't be a goofball, Corrales. Whose country is this? It's a show of friendship.'

Corrales snorted. 'Well, I ain't doing no curtsying.'

Dalinsky cut in. 'Hey, Corrales, and I heard they were going to invite you to tea! And then maybe introduce you to one of their daughters. They're both pretty cute.'

'Very funny. And when they pass by, why don't you ask the king if you can take his eldest daughter out on the town?'

The whole airbase came out to welcome General Eaker's plane. Kittering addressed them all beforehand. There was even a USAAF brass band bussed in for the occasion. As they stood there in the fresh autumn air, waiting for the VIP arrivals, Harry began to get into the spirit of the occasion. There was something glorious about a big parade, and that brass band was pretty good – as good as anything they heard on the radio.

When Eaker arrived in a green DC-3 and stepped out to 'The Stars and Stripes', all gold braid and medals, Harry actually felt a surge of pride. The king and queen arrived shortly afterwards and he was overcome with curiosity. These guys had been part of a family that had ruled this island since before America existed – the America he knew and understood anyway. Actually, these real-life fairytale characters were pretty normal-looking. The king looked like a decent guy, quite shy and quiet really, and the queen looked elegant in her pearls.

Kittering, Eaker and the royal couple made a stately progress down the rows of flight crews as the brass band played a selection of swing hits Harry knew well. The last time he had heard some of them he had been in his family's kitchen, listening to the radio, and he ached for home.

The VIPs passed by the crew of the *Macey May* and Harry held his breath. They didn't stop, although Harry noticed Kittering giving Corrales a long hard stare. Maybe that's why he didn't say anything. The colonel was a hard-ass, but Harry guessed Corrales wouldn't care. After all, what was the worst thing Kittering could do to him – take him off flying duty?

The *Kansas Kate* boys all stood at the front, and when the inspection was over they had to step up, one by one, to have a medal pinned on their chest by General Eaker. The king and queen had a word with each of them too. Movie cameras filmed the whole thing.

It was a memorable moment – one to cherish, thought Harry. He'd be able to write home to his mom and dad about this. The day he – almost – met the King and Queen of England. They had been so close he could have touched them.

But when it was over and they'd all been told to stand easy, Harry felt a nagging unease about the whole thing. He couldn't put it into words, but when he went to the mess that evening John said something that helped him realise what it was.

'Jeezus, the king and queen, and General Eaker, and the whole frigging movie industry. You know what that means, Harry? It means that one of these crews finishing a tour is rare as rocking-horse crap. Ya don't think these guys spend their whole lives going round airbases congratulating crews who've completed twenty-five missions, do you?'

It was something that Harry hadn't really thought about. But it made sense. Even if the royal couple spent all their days sitting around in chintzy drawing rooms, sipping tea and talking about horses, he was sure as hell that General Eaker was a busy man. This was a very rare event.

There was about as much chance of Harry having General Eaker pin one of those medals on him as there was of him marrying Princess Elizabeth. He thought of his brother David and whispered to himself, 'Come and meet me if it turns out bad. Be there, please.' Harry didn't really believe in an afterlife, but if he was going down in a spiralling Fortress he knew in his bones he'd be praying for one then.

The next day Harry was walking over to the mess with John for lunch when he saw a lone Fortress taxiing along to Runway A. A small group of servicemen had gathered at the foot of the runway, and as the plane turned to face the wind, they could see it was *Kansas Kate*. As the engines gathered power the men on the ground unveiled a handful of flags and began to wave. They were cheering and shouting, but the noise they made was completely drowned out by the roar of the B-17's engines.

As Harry stood on the concrete outside the mess hall that early autumn day, he would have given almost anything to have been aboard that plane.

CHAPTER 10

September 21st, 1943

They picked up the rumour of an imminent mission in the canteen at lunchtime on September 21st. Dalinsky said Benik had told him his boys were going to be up all night. When he'd pressed him for more details, the ground crew chief just winked. 'Careless talk costs lives,' he'd said. 'Especially mine if I got caught telling you.'

From that moment on, Harry felt like he was in a dream. He still spoke and breathed and walked around, but the world no longer seemed real. In a strange kind of way he felt he had already left it. He found it almost impossible to sleep that night, and when they were called for their preflight briefing in the early morning, it was as though he was watching a film. Kittering appeared with a handful of other brass, striding through a dense fog of cigarette smoke, and told them they were going to Münster to bomb the rail yards. It was a relatively short run, just inside the German border, and both flak and fighter attacks were expected to be light.

'I bet they say that before every mission,' whispered Corrales.

Harry and the rest of the crew emerged into one of those fresh mornings where you could see your breath and your lungs smarted with the cold bright air, but it would be warmer later.

They went through the usual routine of collecting their high-altitude flight suits, and then queuing at the armoury for their Browning machine guns. In all that time, Harry didn't remember a single conversation he'd had with anyone. People spoke to him and he replied, but nothing was going in. John Hill was the same - totally non-communicative. Corrales, on the other hand, couldn't stop yakking away. And Dalinsky and Skaggs. Fear obviously affected them in different ways.

As they assembled at the *Macey May* Holberg beckoned them all together, and when he suggested a moment for silent prayer before embarking, those of the crew who had a faith bent their heads. Harry remained silent, his eyes lowered out of respect.

A few minutes later they were all inside the plane and Harry wondered if his feet would ever touch solid earth again.

Everything became very real again when the squadron had taken off and they were up over East Anglia, manoeuvring into formation. All at once those droning engines seemed to break into his trance and he was there in his turret, looking down over the lower levels of the combat box - the tight formation bomb groups adopted to give them the best protection from fighter attack. It was a comfort, being part of a massive phalanx of so many Flying Fortresses. They had joined with several nearby squadrons and there must have been over a hundred bombers all heading for the coast.

Harry was sat bunched up inside his turret with his back curved against the padded hatch, his feet curled level with his head. They were flying over Norwich now, and he had the best view on the ship. Ahead, the elegant spire of the cathedral glowed pink in the bright early autumn sunshine.

It had turned into the kind of afternoon where you could go to the park and play ball until the sun started to sink low in the sky and a chill would fill the air to remind you that summer was gone and winter was on the way.

That brought him up short. Now they were on operations, 'tomorrow', 'next week', even 'later', no longer existed. Until they finished their tour, they were suspended in a perpetual 'maybe'.

Holberg's voice cut into Harry's thoughts. 'Look at that, boys. What a beautiful piece of architecture . . .'

Harry fancied he could hear some sniggering from some of the other guys; it was difficult to tell with those four engines roaring away either side of him. But Bortz sighed wearily and cut in, 'Knock it off, you Neanderthals.' Bortz was a pretty pious guy. Never swore. Never made lewd comments about the Women's Auxiliary Air Force girls they sometimes saw around the base.

Holberg ignored it all, although Harry thought he could hear a smile in his voice. 'Norwich Cathedral – eight hundred years old. Probably took them a hundred years to build. Well, it'll still be here when we get back, so don't get too distracted. Fritz could have a few prowling fighters, even here. We hit the enemy coast at ten hundred hours, so that's when you have to really start paying attention. Be ready to test your guns as soon as we cross the coast. I want you all to fire on command, so make sure everything's set.'

Holberg had already told them all this as they waited on their hardstand. Maybe he was just as nervous as the rest of them and needed to be doing something to occupy his mind.

Norwich Cathedral receded in the haze, along with the golden stone of the great castle keep in the centre of the city, and Harry wondered if he would get to see them again on their return journey that afternoon. His gut tightened. That was another 'maybe'.

As they settled into their flight, Holberg asked Skaggs to tune into the BBC Home Service and patch it through the interphone. They liked hearing those Limey voices, all calm and civilised, and the Brits were as keen on swing as the Yanks. 'Chattanooga Choo Choo' came on and they all sang along . . . followed by other dance hall favourites like 'Sleepy Lagoon' and 'Tangerine'.

The Fortress continued to climb. Harry pressed his right foot on the turret control and spun round a full 360 degrees. His left foot moved him up and down. Suspended at 90 degrees, he looked straight down on to the ploughed fields of Norfolk, thousands of feet below.

He wondered how long it would take him to fall if the main shaft holding his turret failed.

A tingling in his arms reminded him he had been dangling down for too long and he moved the turret to the horizontal. Being in his natural position relative to gravity made him feel like a fetus in the womb – like those diagrams in the biology textbooks. But this little steel ball floating in freezing cold air was no cosy haven. Instead of the reassuring rhythm of a heartbeat there was only the ominous drone of engines, an insistent soundtrack that seemed to imply that something terrible was about to happen.

Stearley's voice came over the interphone. 'We're at ten thousand feet. Oxygen on.'

Harry hooked himself up to his leather mask without even thinking about it. He noticed an immediate difference, even though he hadn't been aware of the lack of oxygen before. It was like a noise you only noticed when it stopped. He understood at once how easy it had been for Cain not to have realised his supply had failed. At once he felt more alert and more comfortable. He even felt warmer.

Just after they crossed the Norfolk coast, Stearley came on again to tell them to test their guns. Harry heard John Hill and Ralph Dalinsky fire above him in the waist. When Jim Corrales fired, he could feel the ship rattle but the guns were drowned out by the engines. And all he could tell of the forward guns was a slight extra vibration above the usual rattle and lurch of a B-17 in flight.

Everything went quiet after that, save for the regular oxygen checks, so routine Harry barely registered them.

Holberg interrupted the silence. 'Enemy coast twenty minutes.' This was it. The hairs on the back of his neck stood on end.

As the minutes slipped away Harry shifted uncomfortably and wished he had not had to jam that folded-up copy of the *East Anglia Courier* in his back pocket. Next time he'd leave it with his parachute in the main fuselage. He wriggled his left leg, to relieve the cramp that was building, and accidently touched the foot pedal. The turret lurched a full 180 degrees and there he was staring straight at the French coast. From this distance it looked like any old coastline but as they grew nearer, and other aircraft ahead of them in the combat box came within range, enemy flak positions along the seashore began to open up. Harry saw flashes on the ground and then puffs of black smoke exploding in the air ahead. They looked like little balls of dirty cotton wool. His stomach gave a lurch and everything inside him tightened.

'Look at that,' he wanted to shout. 'Those bastards down there are trying to kill us.' All at once he felt terribly lonely. Him and Jim Corrales back at the end of the plane, they had the worst jobs. Not the most difficult – Harry knew the pilots and the navigator were pretty much occupied all the time – but at least the rest of the crew had each other for company. They had someone else to look at for comfort, someone else to help them if their oxygen mask failed, or, God forbid, they got hit by flak or bullets from a Nazi fighter. Harry and Jim could sit there and bleed to death and no one would know.

There was a sudden jolt, the kind you got when you hit an air pocket, and Harry was buffeted around in his little steel world. His courage was deserting him fast. For the first time ever, he felt really trapped in there. Now he was faced with the reality of actual enemy action, he was painfully aware of the danger he was in.

Holberg had told Harry there would be times when no fighters would come swooping in, not least when they were going through heavy flak, and he would tell him when he could come back into the plane. Harry wondered if he'd remembered.

On cue, the interphone crackled. It was Holberg. 'Friedman, you can come out of your turret. But get back in as soon as I tell you.'

'Thank you, Captain.' Harry was out of there in a frenzied minute of unbuckling, unplugging, caught straps, awkward wriggling . . . he almost forgot to lock the turret in the 90-degree down position and only remembered as he reached for the catch that opened the hatch out into the fuselage. John and Ralph Dalinsky immediately appeared to haul him out.

It was utterly illogical, but Harry felt safer now he was with the two waist gunners. He stood behind Dalinsky, peering out at the coast through the right window. There were occasional bursts of flak around them now, not just ahead.

The smell of high explosives caught in his throat. It was strangely reminiscent of nail varnish.

The *Macey May* bucked in the air, and Harry was thrown to the floor, his head narrowly missing the sharp corner of an ammunition box. 'You have to hold on tight here, Harry,' John shouted in his ear as he pulled him to his feet.

Harry began to feel light-headed and a little nauseous. He wondered for a moment if he'd been hit, but dismissed the idea. He'd have felt it surely? Then he suddenly realised that he had forgotten to pick up one of the little oxygen bottles and masks placed at intervals around the ship for crew members who had to move away from their usual station. He looked around to locate the nearest one, but there was a sudden loud explosion and the plane shook violently. Then another. And another. The *Macey May* was bucking around like a car speeding through a ploughed field. They were in the thick of it now. He could see it all around them through both waist windows.

The Perspex left side window shattered into thousands of fragments and he almost jumped out of his skin. Then it disintegrated before their eyes, blown in by the force of the slipstream. The temperature dropped in an instant and the great roaring sound of the engines became overwhelming.

There were sharp little pinging noises, loud enough to hear even over those engines, and Harry could see little holes in the thin skin of the fuselage behind them where pencil-thin beams of sunlight poured in. He looked at John and Ralph in their flak aprons – heavy steel plates almost like medieval armour – and felt totally vulnerable there in the waist with no protection at all. Those holes had been made by razor-sharp fragments of flak passing through the *Macey May*. They would have passed straight through him too, if he'd been standing there.

He remembered Ernie telling them how fragile the skin of the Fortress was. Its strength lay in those concentric rings and the struts that formed the frame of the aircraft. The thin aluminium plates kept the wind out – but you could punch through those with a little screwdriver.

Harry crouched down, as if to make himself smaller, and clutched desperately at one of the rings that made up the inner structure of the fuselage. Every breath, every movement, was forced. He could feel his heart thumping in his chest and wondered if each beat would be his last.

The explosions were less frequent now and Harry started to come out of his own terror-filled bubble. He realised he was drenched in sweat and could feel his hands swimming around inside his thick gloves. As sweat cooled on his exposed face he noticed how cold it was in the waist. But the deep drone of those Wright Cyclone engines was steady enough, so at least they hadn't been hit. Were the others OK, he began to wonder. He could see John and Ralph were both standing up. They must be all right.

'Hey, Harry,' he heard John call out to him. 'Where's your oxygen?' John grabbed a bottle of oxygen and made his way towards him.

Harry placed the mask over his face and immediately began to feel better. A strange elation overcame him. 'We made it. We frigging made it. We're still here,' he shouted.

He looked up, realised no one was paying him any attention, and felt grateful he was not plugged into the interphone.

'Harry, Captain says back in your ball,' shouted Ralph over the roar of inrushing air.

'You OK?' Harry asked, a big grin now plastered over his face.

Ralph gestured towards the shattered left window. 'I'm glad of this heated suit,' he shouted.

Harry paused to slap John on the back and then wriggled back into his turret. As soon as he plugged himself back into the interphone he heard Holberg's voice. 'That flak was pretty intense and no one went down. That's got to be good news. Well done, boys.'

This had been his first test. His first time under fire. He had got through it.

But as he was strapping himself in to the harness in his turret he noticed a long clean cut in his flying jacket, just at the side and down to his waist – almost like someone had taken a swipe at it with those tailor's scissors with the long blades. Something had flown past and missed him by a whisker. A fragment of flak that could have sprayed his guts all over the waist.

When he felt able to speak again, Harry told Holberg he was back in his turret. The patchwork countryside of occupied France rolled by far beneath his feet. Down there were real, actual Nazis. The thought of what the Nazis were doing gave him courage. This was worth it. It was terrifying, and they might all be killed. But at least he was getting back at the Nazis.

Holberg, his voice calm and steady, came over the interphone. 'You boys at the back, and underneath, you listening? Friedman? Corrales?'

'Copy.' They both grunted an acknowledgement.

'Keep sweeping the sky, top to bottom. Skaggs and Lieutenant Bortz, you keep our front covered. Dalinsky, Hill, watch our flanks. If we keep a tight defensive formation – and this combat box is looking pretty good – we should be able to swat anything that tries to dive through us. And all of you, if those fighters do come, watch you don't go hitting our own ships in all the excitement.'

If the fighters come. Judging by the canteen talk, there was never a mission when the fighters didn't come. Harry continued to roll his turret around the sky, up and down, all angles. Sometimes he'd see little black dots and wonder if it was just eye strain.

This waiting for the fighters was terrible. Harry almost began to wish they would show up so he could stop worrying about them coming.

Holberg came on to tell them they were an hour away from Münster and then things would get a lot rougher.

The hour passed so slowly Harry checked several times to make sure his wristwatch hadn't stopped. There were several alerts, when members of the crew thought they could see enemy fighters in the distance, but none of these turned out to be the real thing.

'OK, here comes trouble,' Holberg said over the interphone. 'Hold tight, boys. Flak looks pretty heavy couple of miles ahead. Bortz, five minutes, then it's over to you.'

In less than a minute the *Macey May* started to buck again. Harry kept waiting for the captain to tell him when he could come out, but Holberg had other things on his mind. So Harry did what he was supposed to do and swung the turret round a constant 360-degree rotation in case any Kraut fighter pilots were mad enough to engage them in the middle of their own flak field.

Ahead in the combat box, Harry saw the leading bombers open their bomb doors. Through the clouds he could see the grey shape of a conurbation below – houses, office buildings, hospitals . . . and the scar of a great railway marshalling yard. The sun caught on a large body of water to the centre west of the city. It didn't seem real, what they were about to destroy.

Then the *Macey May*'s own bomb doors opened in front of him. Holberg came over. 'Bortz, the ship is yours.' That was standard procedure. On a bomb run the bombardier took control of the plane from his station at the nose and could make his own minor corrections to the flight path.

The flak grew to a crescendo and Harry realised he actually felt safer curled up in his little ball, especially when he thought of John and Ralph, standing up in the waist above him.

The leading bombers began to drop their loads. There was something animalistic about it – as though they were emptying their bowels – shitting over enemy territory. He watched those little green bombs whistle down, wobbling as they did in deadly clusters of ten. This was something he had never seen before, and what shocked him the most was the sheer violence of their detonation. As each cluster landed, the ground would disappear at random moments microseconds apart. Even from twenty-five thousand feet up he could see the shock waves as they exploded and the plumes of smoke and dust that erupted around them.

Just ahead in the combat box to the left of them there was a sudden flash – bright enough to make Harry flinch. He saw a Fortress explode in an instant into great clouds of yellow and red flame and tendrils of black oily smoke.

'Jesus Christ,' came a voice over the interphone. Harry didn't know who it belonged to, but they sounded utterly terrified.

The explosion hung in the air for a moment, as pieces of debris arced through the sky. Apart from the tail section, which was still intact, there wasn't anything else recognisable as a Flying Fortress.

'Bortz, drop those bombs, for Chrissakes.' That was Dalinsky, crackling in Harry's earpiece. He was utterly wrong to speak and Holberg rapidly admonished him with a curt 'Silence in the waist'.

But Harry could see why he was so concerned. A direct hit by flak on a plane full of bombs was a catastrophe none of them would survive. In training they had been told they always stood a chance if their Fortress went down. Not with a full payload they didn't.

Another Fortress to the right of them began to trail smoke from both right engines. Then the whole wing caught – a dense yellow and black stream of flame and black smoke. The plane dropped out of formation and began its shallow dive to earth.

'Come on, guys, come on, get out of there,' Harry heard in his earpiece. He willed them to bail out too, totally distracted from the bomb run and the flak. Three black specks fell from the Fortress and white parachutes blossomed in the sky. Then there was a sudden bright flash as the wing fuel tanks ignited and the stricken Fortress began a dizzying spin, like a great metal leaf whirling to earth. Once that happened you were doomed – pinned to your stations by centrifugal force, like a fairground ride in hell.

'Bombs away,' said Bortz, as the *Macey May* lifted in the air, suddenly free of its 4,500-pound load. Harry spun his turret round to watch those ten green pods plummet from the bomb bay, rapidly lagging behind the aircraft as the *Macey May* powered on through the sky.

Another Fortress began trailing smoke from its left outer engine. That was quickly extinguished but then the propeller stopped rotating. It was the *Carolina Peach*. Harry had shared meals with their non-coms on several occasions.

Holberg came over the interphone. 'We're on our way home. Watch out for fighters.'

Harry felt a familiar squirming in his stomach. They must come, surely. Didn't they always? He managed to stay awake for the return flight and wished there was something to distract him from the plummeting bombers and the flak fragment that had nearly ripped his stomach open. It was exhausting staring into endless, empty sky. Some music would have been good, but Holberg turned down Corrales' request for the BBC Home Service.

'Sorry, Jim,' he said. 'I want you all to keep your eyes open. We're all tired. We're all a bit jittery. We're over the worst, but I don't want some Nazi fighter to creep up on us just when we think we're safe.'

For the first half-hour of the journey home, *Carolina Peach*, the Fortress that had lost an engine over Münster, had managed to keep up with them, lagging only a little behind the tail end of the combat box. But as he scanned the sky for fighters, Harry also noticed it gradually losing height. The inner left engine began to flame too and trail black smoke, but the pilot was obviously still in control. No parachutes appeared.

'Godspeed, boys,' Harry heard Holberg say. 'Maybe they'll get back if they're lucky with the fighters.'

As the minutes ticked away, the grey North Sea appeared on the horizon and Harry began to hope they would not be attacked after all.

Fighters did come – their own escort. Just as they reached the coast two squadrons of Lightnings arrived and flew above the combat box. The Germans rarely attacked when the bombers had their own fighters to protect them. Harry felt an overwhelming relief. They had done it. They had flown their first combat mission and survived. He felt a surge of pride in his crew.

The bomb group were back at Kirkstead by 3 p.m. No one crashed on landing, although a couple of the bombers fired their flares on approach, alerting the ambulance crews they had badly injured men aboard.

As they emerged from the main exit at the rear of the Fortress, Ernie was there to greet them, along with the rest of his crew. He waited for all ten of them to appear, and then his face broke into a wide grin.

Holberg came over and gave him a slap on the back. 'Hey, Ernie. We would never have known the difference!' He turned to the other ground crew, who had gathered around. 'Thanks, boys. She flew like a dream. And to tell you the truth, the number four ran even better than on the old *Macey May*.'

In the canteen afterwards they discovered the B-17 that had exploded over Münster was one of theirs. It had been on its first mission too. Harry felt glad he didn't know any of them. There was no news on *Carolina Peach*. Harry hoped the guys had managed to parachute out before the plane was too low for a safe escape.

They also heard there had been a massive raid on Frankfurt. Maybe that was where all the Kraut fighters had gone.

Skaggs knew at once what had happened. 'We were a decoy raid. The Krauts had their hands full with the Frankfurt bomber stream. Lucky it wasn't the other way round.'

CHAPTER 11

After a hot shower Harry went over to the canteen to eat his evening meal. Now they had recovered from the flight, the crews were all bluster and wisecracks, and talked about their mission over their steak dinner, careful not to mention the guys who had been lost. Harry began to relax.

He shared a table with John and Ralph and Jim and they all agreed it hadn't been that bad and that Holberg had been superb. 'We've got a great crew,' said John. 'Even Bortz and Stearley. They're stuck-up jerks sometimes, but they do their job pretty good.'

Now the exhaustion and tension of the raid had worn off Harry was in high spirits. 'Ernie Benik's boys did a great job on the new plane,' he said. 'If anything's going to get us through these twenty-five missions, I'm sure it'll be the *Macey May*.'

Sitting in the corner of their table, a staff sergeant eyed them with indifference. He seemed quite despondent, but maybe he was just the quiet type. Harry thought he ought to bring him into the conversation. 'Were you over Münster today?' he asked him.

'Yep, mission number nine. You boys were on your first, weren't you? I can tell.'

They all nodded.

'I wish you luck. We're in the waiting room to hell here. Those other guys that never came back, they just caught an earlier train. We all catch that train sooner or later.'

'What about those guys in *Kansas Kate*?' John Hill said indignantly. 'They did OK. They got through their twenty-five!'

The sergeant just looked at him, then got up to leave. 'Like I say, I wish you luck.'

When he was out of earshot Corrales put an arm around Harry. 'Hey, buddy. Rule number one. Don't talk to strangers. Didn't your momma ever tell you?'

'Miserable loser,' spat John. 'We're gonna be OK. I'll bet any of you fifty bucks we'll be still here after our twenty-five.'

They cheered and walked off, arms around one another's shoulders. Holberg waylaid them as they reached the hut. 'Good news, boys, we've got passes off the base tomorrow night. I'm taking you into the village. A few pints of that warm Limey beer in the Green Man. That'll do us good.'

They all met up at the main gates of the base that next evening and walked down to the village in ten minutes. The Green Man was a solid brick inn with Dutch gables. Harry guessed it was at least two or three hundred years old, built back when the settlers in the US were living in barely more than wooden cabins. The buildings were something which endlessly fascinated him here in England.

That night the pub was nicely crowded and a roaring log fire took the chill off the early autumn evening. They found two tables next to each other, officers on one, non-coms on the other. Holberg went to buy the beers and they all rubbed along well enough, although Bortz and LaFitte kept an obvious distance.

Two RAF junior officers came to sit in their corner of the pub and they fell into easy conversation. They introduced themselves as Gordon and Ray and said they had cycled over from the British base at Woodton. Harry liked these guys and they made him roar with laughter, especially after he had had a couple of pints of that English beer.

The Limeys were talking about their commander-in-chief, a brusque rather stern-looking man known as 'Bomber Harris' in the newspapers, although Harry had heard the British flyers called him 'Butcher Harris'.

'He has a suite at Claridge's,' Ray told them, referring to a posh London hotel. 'That's where he spends his life, being pampered by WAAF girls. They fuss around him peeling grapes and stuffing foie gras into his mouth. And when he tires of that, he picks up a gold-plated telephone and commands us to go on a mission.'

'Yes, he does, it's true,' said Gordon, 'and when we get back a list of our exploits is read out to him as he soaks in a warm bath of champagne. If he's particularly impressed, he has one of his servants pick up a gold pen and writes a letter on vellum to our CO . . .'

'. . . in purple ink,' butted in Ray.

'. . . recommending us for a medal.'

Gordon and Ray made them all laugh, even the officers. For a few hours that night, Harry completely forgot he was a ball turret gunner on active service.

Harry's night out was complete when the pub filled up with a group of noisy girls, just off the evening shift at a nearby factory, by the look of their overalls and head-scarves. When he went to buy the guys a drink, he found himself standing next to a familiar face at the bar. He recognised Tilly at once, and even in her factory clothes he still thought she looked beautiful. He asked if he could buy her a drink.

'You came for tea with Grandma,' she said. 'Harry, isn't it? Did you send your trinkets back home?'

Harry admitted he hadn't. He wanted to tell her about the extraordinary things that had happened to him since he had last seen her, but he wasn't sure if it was all supposed to be a secret so instead he asked her what she had been doing. Tilly worked in the sugar beet factory five days a week – 'You come home just coated in this musty sweet stink. You must have noticed the smell from the factory at the airbase when the wind's blowing that way.'

When he asked about her family, she told him she had a brother who flew Lancaster bombers out of Waddington in Lincolnshire.

'Whoops, shouldn't have told you that,' she said, clasping a hand to her mouth. 'All this "Careless talk costs lives" is so annoying. We're supposed to treat everyone like a spy. You don't look like a spy to me.'

Harry told her the story about Bomber Harris and the gold-plated telephone. She roared with laughter and said she couldn't wait to tell Colin. 'That's his name, but I suppose that's a secret too.'

John came up to the bar. 'Hey, Harry, where are the drinks?' he said and smiled broadly at them both, then ordered another round for the non-coms. Harry was pleased he didn't try to join them and just as pleased to see Tilly had practically ignored him.

As the evening ended she asked him if he had been to Norwich yet. Harry said how much he'd like to explore the city, having seen it from the air.

'I know just the person to show you around.'

Harry sensed she was playing with him and wondered if she was going to suggest her grandma.

'Next time you're on leave at the weekend, drop off a note with my grandmother, and I'll take you.'

Harry floated back to base on a cloud. Maybe it was the beer, but he felt euphoric. He couldn't believe his luck. That night he fell asleep with a smile on his lips.

CHAPTER 12

Westerschelde, Occupied Netherlands,
September 24th, 1943

Feldwebel Richter could see the tail of the Fortress just poking over the breaking waves in the outgoing tide – a splash of red and silver in a grey sea and grey sky. He shivered and pulled his Wehrmacht greatcoat tight around his collar. A fierce wind whipped in from the north, sweeping over the deck of the salvage vessel. It was dreary out here, still and silent save for the splash of waves and the mournful cry of gulls. It was a place of the dead. Richter could see the apprehension on the faces of his salvage squad, but he had been told this was valuable work and it had to be done.

The Fortress had crash-landed in the shallow waters of the Westerschelde, north-west of Antwerp, on the way back from that raid on the marshalling yards at Münster.

It took at least an hour for the diver and the lifting crew to attach heavy canvas straps to the wings and raise the plane out of the murky shallows. But once they had got it to the surface they had only to steam a few yards further to deposit it on the exposed mudflats of the tidal zone.

With a creaking and grinding of metal, the rear of the fuselage snapped as the Fortress settled into the muddy beach. Water flooded out in a torrent, and in smaller streams and rivulets from the many other holes that peppered the front part of the fuselage.

As soon as the craft broke surface Richter could see the pilot and co-pilot were still in the cockpit. He wondered if any of the others had got out. He noted the name too – *Carolina Peach* – and a garish painting of a semi-naked girl with wavy blonde hair.

A thin drizzle started to settle in and the *Feldwebel* reached for another cigarette to take his mind off the task ahead. The Dutch captain came over and told him in broken German that he and his men had about half an hour to recover the bodies before the tide came in to reclaim the downed bomber.

So Feldwebel Richter and his squad boarded the small sailboat that came attached to the barge and were swiftly ferried the short distance to the wrecked aircraft.

Richter was first in, entering through the broken rear section. The first thing he saw was the body of one of the crew, hand still clasped around the handle of the rear exit door. He was almost certainly a gunner, judging by the sergeant rank visible on his sodden uniform. A small man, Richter noticed, with matted blond hair. He looked like an Aryan, one of the master race.

The rest of the crew were there – all ten of them. No one had bailed out. Most were in a jumble of arms and legs in the radio operator's compartment. It was an unpleasant business, untangling this soaking human knot, but it could have been far worse. The Fortress had only been in the sea a day or two, and decomposition had barely begun.

One by one they brought the bodies out to lay them on the shore. The pilot and co-pilot were the most difficult to extract and they had dropped both of them as they struggled through the cramped, cluttered interior.

They looked peaceful enough, Richter supposed, and imagined all of them had been killed or knocked unconscious when their Fortress crashed into the sea. They said the sea was as hard as a brick wall if you came down too fast. The one at the rear door had nearly made it out, but it had jammed by the look of it. Richter almost felt a stab of pity for the man. But then he remembered the mess Allied bombers had made of his home town of Hamburg and thought no more about it.

When they had all the dead men out they ferried them over to the barge and chugged south-east with the incoming tide to Antwerp. On the journey back Richter's men completed the melancholy task of removing all the clothes from the bodies, from flying helmets to socks and underwear.

The deathly white corpses were loaded into a van that took them straight to Antwerp's crematorium. Their clothes were washed and ironed and sent to Gestapo headquarters at Prinz-Albrecht-Strasse in Berlin.

CHAPTER 13

Kirkstead, East Anglia, October 1st, 1943

At five o' clock in the morning, Ernie Benik arrived with a thermos of fresh coffee. There was a briefing at six. Harry had a thick head. It had been the Jewish New Year the night before, and most of the Jewish guys on the base had met up to celebrate. Harry had enjoyed himself, but the evening left him aching for home.

Just as the *Macey May*'s non-coms were entering the briefing hut, Stearley dashed up to them.

'We've got a passenger,' he said.

They stared uneasily, awaiting the rest of the news.

'That news guy, Eddie Burnet. You might have seen him hanging around the base these last couple of days. He's coming with us.'

'Says who?' Corrales could barely contain his amazement.

'Look, boys, this is straight from the top. Gotta go.'

The *Macey May*'s non-coms shuffled into the briefing room, muttering to themselves.

When the curtain over the map of Europe was drawn back to reveal the target, a concerned murmur rippled around the room. They were going to Stuttgart to bomb the factories there. They'd all heard the stories. Barely a month ago, an Eighth Air Force raid on the city had cost them nearly fifty bombers. The city was deep in southern Germany. It was going to be a long flight.

Kittering finished his briefing and then called for the crew of the *Macey May* to remain behind when the rest of the men had been dismissed. He drew heavily on his cigarette and his words came out in a cascade of smoke.

'You've all seen Eddie Burnet around the station. He's telling the folks back home about what brave boys you all are and how you're helping to win the war. Eddie was going up with *Sally D*, but ground crew are still working on her. I thought you *Macey May* fellas would do instead. He's got orders not to get in your way, but if you smile sweetly he'll take your pictures and tell all the readers of *Life* magazine what a bunch of heroes you are.'

Kittering cast a flinty eye at the tall figure of Corrales at the back of the group with his peaked cap perched right at the back of his head. 'I expect you all to behave in an exemplary fashion for the benefit of your passenger.' Then he dismissed them too. 'OK, on your way, and Godspeed.'

The *Macey May*'s non-coms shuffled out of the door. The sun had come out and the sky was now almost cloudless.

'Looking good. Blue sky's no place to hide a Messerschmitt,' said John.

'So what about Burnet?' said Ralph Dalinsky.

'I bet Stearley's wetting his pants with excitement,' said Skaggs. 'I seen him buttering Burnet up. He's probably thinking he'll get even more ladies chasing after him if he had his picture in *Life* magazine.'

'Hey, maybe that'll work for us all!' Corrales said. 'Maybe we will be all over *Life* magazine. My mama reads that. She'll be showing it to all the neighbours.'

They all took a final trip to the latrine, then suited up. 'Hey, Harry, we're going to be fine,' said John as he zipped up his heavy fur-lined boots. 'The news guy, he's famous. I read him since I was a kid. He was in the Spanish Civil War, and he was at Dunkirk, and then the Blitz. Guy must be invincible!'

Ralph said, 'Last thing he did I saw was interview Clark Gable.'

'I like Gable,' said Coralles. 'He's a gunner, ain't he, over in Polebrook? Hah. Just like us. Anyone that famous who volunteers for this must be crazy!'

'Gable's just doing his duty,' Skaggs said, 'like we all are. I don't give a damn if he's a film star. They ain't special, least no more than anyone else who volunteers to fly combat missions.'

Dalinsky changed the subject. 'I read the news guy too. He interviewed FDR last year.'

'What!' said Harry. 'This guy's interviewed the president! And now he's come to talk to us!'

This was extraordinary. Harry forgot about what they were going to do. He was rubbing shoulders with a man who had met Franklin Delano Roosevelt. His parents were lifelong Democrats. They had a picture of FDR up in the kitchen. They would be over the moon when they heard about this.

The non-coms collected their guns at the armoury, then clambered aboard a jeep that took them across the base to the *Macey May*'s hardstand. The officers were already there, gathered under the nose of the B-17, chatting and smoking with another figure.

'Yup, that's him,' said Skaggs. 'Let's hope he's not a jerk.'

'Hey, boys, come and meet our passenger,' said Holberg.

'Hi, fellas.' Eddie Burnet shook their hands. 'Colonel Kittering told me you'd all take a good photo. That's why he put me in with you.'

The crew scoffed and sniggered in disbelief. The colonel hadn't told them that part.

'It's a great honour to fly with you all. I haven't flown a combat mission before so I have to tell you I'm scared shitless.'

They all chuckled and Harry liked the man at once. He was older than them, maybe in his thirties.

'You do know this is only our second combat mission, right?' said Corrales.

For a second Burnet eye's flickered in surprise. He hid it well enough. 'Great! What a story that'll make.'

* * *

120

Inside the Fortress Harry was struck by the familiar odour of aviation fuel, sweat, lubricating oil, copper wires, a hint of urine. Before, the smell had always been comforting, and a little exciting, but now, going into combat for the second time, he found it unsettling, sinister even.

Once they were off the ground he waited as long as he could before he squeezed into his turret. He wanted Eddie to interview him. Sure enough, as they climbed above the Norfolk landscape, the journalist made his way down the fuselage.

'Christ, it's noisy in here!'

'Better talk to Harry first,' shouted John. 'He's gotta get into his turret any minute.'

Harry grinned. John had read his mind.

'So what's it like in there, Sergeant?'

Harry thought for a while. Should he be honest and tell him it was claustrophobic and he often had nightmares about being trapped, or crushed to death if he couldn't get out and the Fortress had to do a belly landing? Or should he lie?

He lied.

'Great piece of machinery, sir,' said Harry. 'You slide in and then everything moves around smooth as you like. None of them Messerschmitts are gonna get past me!'

'That's the spirit, son,' said Burnet. 'Now, where you from?'

'Brooklyn, sir.'

'No kidding. I'm just across the water.'

'Whereabouts?'

'Lexington Avenue. Chrysler Building.'

It was the most exclusive address in New York.

'You can probably see into our apartment windows!' Harry joked.

'No kidding,' said Burnet again. 'You on the river front?'

'Almost.'

Harry had watched that skyscraper go up when he was a kid. 'Hey, here we are,' he said. 'You living in the most beautiful building in the world, me in the most beautiful plane in the world.'

He hoped the journalist would write that down, but he didn't.

Harry meant it. He loved the B-17. It was the most elegant, magnificent machine he had ever seen.

'Let's have a shot of you getting in your turret,' said Burnet. 'I wanna get as many shots off as I can before we get too high. I've been warned things might freeze up above fifteen thousand feet.'

Harry felt pleased with himself. Burnet had spoken to him, and now he wanted a pic. That was something his mom and dad would be proud to show to all their friends.

Harry anchored the turret in its straight-down position and opened the hatch. For a moment he even forgot that pit of the stomach fear he usually felt, levering himself into that little bubble thousands of feet above the surface of the earth.

'No parachute, huh?' said Burnet.

'No space,' said Harry.

'You worry about that?' asked Burnet.

'No, sir,' he lied. 'My buddies will help me out if we get into trouble.'

Harry squeezed down, stopping to give a thumbs-up and a grin when he was halfway in. Then he snapped the lid down, taking extra care to ensure the latches were locked tight. He pressed the control buttons and felt the mechanism respond with a reassuring swiftness. That was it. He was alone now, until Holberg told him he could get out.

Harry smiled. For a moment this strange turn of events had taken their minds off an awful truth. But then it hit him hard. Today was another day when there might not be an afternoon. There might not even be a midday, if they were unlucky.

CHAPTER 14

Above Liège, October 1st, 1943

Hauptmann Heinz Frey peered down from the cockpit of his Messerschmitt 109. He had never got used to that mixture of fear and excitement he felt before an attack. How could you? There you were, ten thousand metres up in the stratosphere, one or two thousand metres higher than the bombers, ready to scream down out of the sun. His airspeed indicator touched 640 kilometres an hour when he did that. It was a phenomenal feeling. Like being one of the gods of ancient times. And then in a matter of seconds the bombers would change from tiny specks streaming white trails to great lumbering machines spitting tracer.

If you were lucky, they crumbled under your cannon fire. You could see sparks and flashes dancing along the wings and fuselage. Sometimes they blew up in front of you, if you hit a bomb or a fuel tank. That was alarming. You could get caught up in that.

Then you would streak past and in a split second you might see the frightened faces of the boys inside. Frey didn't like that. Once he caught a glimpse inside the cockpit of a Fortress he had hit and there was a pilot sitting there in his brown leather jacket, his head missing. The co-pilot staring straight ahead. At that moment Frey had felt an overwhelming desire to throw up into his oxygen mask. But he managed to hold it down. You had to be careful as you dived through the formations – 'combat boxes', he had heard they called them. A split second's bad timing, a momentary twitch of the joystick in the wrong direction, and you could collide and both of you would be engulfed in a great fireball. He had seen that happen a couple of times.

Like many of his comrades he was a veteran from the Russian front. They didn't usually make those kinds of mistakes. But the older pilots like him, the ones who had reached their mid-twenties, were slowly disappearing and being replaced by fresh-faced young boys. The new ones were full of Nazi zeal, but that didn't make up for experience.

Something else you noticed too, when you dived through the formations, were the pictures the Americans painted on the noses of their bombers. Nudes, or at least the scantiest clad girls imaginable. Frey sometimes wondered if these pictures were a deliberate ploy by the Americans to put the fighter pilots off their aim. The Propaganda and Enlightenment officials of the Luftwaffe had given them a talk recently and one political officer had told them these 'obscene paintings' were an obvious sign of the decadence of that 'cesspit of a mongrel nation'.

But Frey had a sneaking regard for these Yankee pilots. Theirs was a terrifying job, and, like him, they were doing their duty. He was glad it wasn't him stuck in one of those lumbering machines, although even he could admit that the Fortresses were beautiful-looking aircraft. He even went to talk to them sometimes, if they crashed near his airbase. They were OK. Decent men in the main. A few had come from German stock and had even spoken to him like natives. They were careful not to talk politics on those occasions.

Now here he was ready to dive, almost wing to wing with his *Schwarm* of three other fighters, the sun warm on the back of his flying helmet. They were seconds away from it. Frey's mouth was desperately dry but he resisted the temptation to reach for his water bottle and have a final swig. He might miss the formation leader's signal to go.

The lead Messerschmitt tilted its wings and dived. The rest of the *Jagdgeschwader* followed behind with well-trained precision. There were fifty of them in that fighter group, up in the sky that morning. They had missed the bomber stream on the way in. That had been a great pity and deprived them of the opportunity to down these beasts before they dropped their bombs, but they would make sure plenty of the huge machines didn't get home.

Frey was set to squeeze off his first volley and waited until the Fortress was bang in the middle of his sight. He felt the fuselage of his tiny Messerschmitt tremble as his machine guns and cannon poured fire into the looming silver bomber. He was too busy concentrating to really notice whether his shots hit home, too concerned to make sure he flew between the gaps in the tight combat box formation.

Frey came out of his dive, the G-forces pinning him hard to his seat and making even the simple action of pulling back the control stick a matter of sheer strength. He realised he was soaked in cold sweat and waited a few seconds for his head to clear. A B-17 near his target had exploded dangerously close as he made his pass.

As he prepared to climb again for another go at the bombers he noticed his controls were sluggish. The engine was misfiring and something was clearly not right. Heinz Frey was not a coward, but he knew when it was time to leave the field of battle. He radioed his commander to tell him what had happened. Then he turned his Messerschmitt away from the bomber stream and headed for the nearest airbase. He was not going to throw his life away in a failing machine, and if he was lucky his fighter would be easily repaired and ready for the next assault. It was a shame, he reflected, that he had not caused any significant damage.

CHAPTER 15

In the nose, Bortz had followed the diving Messerschmitt all the way in, realising at least seven seconds before he fired that this one had the *Macey May* in its sites. But Bortz had never really mastered the intricacies of the remote-controlled Bendix chin turret. Even in training, his aim had been barely acceptable. Bortz was a highly skilled bombardier so they had turned a blind eye to his poor shooting. Cain was there too in the nose, firing one of the single side-guns just beside him.

Burnet stood behind them, just by the passageway up to the cockpit, peering with undisguised fear through the great Plexiglas nose cone, and realising all at once that all that lay between them and Luftwaffe cannon shells and bullets was a transparent plastic shell.

To their right there was a huge explosion. A Fortress next to them had disintegrated and was falling out of the sky. Bortz turned round to Burnet and shouted, 'Did you see that?' but even as the words left his mouth he realised he was talking to a dead man. Burnet lay sprawled across the narrow passage with the top of his head blown off and a look of wide-eyed astonishment on his face. You could see the grey mass of his brain among the bone and hair.

The Messerschmitt swept past the *Macey May*'s right side. Ralph Dalinsky rattled off a volley. The tiny Messerschmitt was too close and going too fast to have any real chance. If he hit anything, it would be a lucky shot. And Dalinsky was sure he hadn't been lucky.

Harry, under the wing, saw the Messerschmitt as it flew away and had more time to get a bead on it. He fired a long burst at the limit of his range and thought he saw something fly off the fighter.

Another Messerschmitt buzzed past almost as fast as the eye could register. Then Harry felt the ship shake and could see fragments flying off the wing close to his turret. The shots had landed right on the fuel tanks and his heart froze as he waited for the wing to catch fire and the Fortress to start to plummet.

'Captain, that last pass caught us on the right wing,' he said.

'Yeah, I saw it too.' The voice was Dalinsky. He sounded as frightened as Harry was feeling. 'Bits were flying everywhere. Could ignite any second.'

'OK, understood.' Holberg's voice was calm and collected. 'Keep looking for fighters. Engines are still running OK. Those tanks are self-sealing. If there was going to be a fire, it would have caught by now.'

Harry didn't know how Holberg managed to keep calm like that.

'Two Fockes, three o' clock low,' cut in Dalinsky again.

That one was for Harry. He spun his turret in an instant and let off a long burst.

Dalinsky was firing too – he was still in his field of vision.

'Watch that ammo, boys,' said Holberg. 'Can't have you running out of bullets while we're still half an hour off our fighter escort.'

The German fighters vanished as swiftly as they had arrived. Harry breathed deep and shivered. He was freezing cold. In all the terror of the moment it had not occurred to him at all. Now here he was, covered in sweat at twenty thousand feet. He felt for the electric plug on his heated suit and realised it had come out of its socket. Once that plug was back in he could feel a life-giving warmth spread throughout his body, thawing his bones.

Harry carried on scanning the skies, but as the adrenalin dropped he began to feel sharp pains in his knees. His flying suit was chafed and there was blood around both knees. At first he though he must have been hit, but quickly worked out what had happened. The gun bolts on either side of his legs had been rubbing against his knees. He had been so caught up in the fighting he hadn't even noticed. They were really starting to throb now, but at least it was just surface bleeding.

'Twenty minutes to the Dutch coast and we should pick up our fighter escort there,' said Stearley.

Bortz spotted the escort first. 'Little friends at one o' clock high. And, hey, we've got the RAF with us too,' he reported. A squadron of Thunderbolts swooped over, turning tightly in the sky, keeping a good two thousand feet above them. Another squadron of Spitfires pulled alongside. Harry had never seen these beautiful planes in flight – just photographs. It felt good to have twenty-four fighters flying with them. It reminded Harry of how he used to feel when he went out with his big brother, knowing he was looking out for him.

Harry Friedman realised he had stopped breathing as Holberg made his final approach. Only when the wheels hit the concrete runway did he draw a deep breath again. The *Macey May* taxied over to her hardstand and the crew piled out to stand on firm ground. Most of the surviving Fortresses were back now, although there was a smouldering pyre at the end of Runway C, close to the hay barn by Grange Farm. Fire trucks were racing towards it, sirens blazing, but from what Harry could see, there wasn't anything for them to do once they got there, except maybe make sure the fire didn't spread to the barn.

He noticed an ambulance heading towards them too, and wondered who on the *Macey May* had been injured. He turned and counted them all – Holberg, Stearley, Bortz, Cain, LaFitte, Skaggs, Hill, Dalinsky, Corrales. They looked tired and sweaty, a little spooked with shock and fatigue even, but none of them was wounded as far as he could see.

'What's this about, sir?' he asked the captain.

Holberg looked grey. 'Burnet's dead. Something took the top of his head off. Let's leave it to the ambulance boys to get him off.'

CHAPTER 16

Kirkstead, East Anglia, October 2nd, 1943

Harry woke up next day to news that had carried all around the English-speaking world. John Hill showed him a copy of *The Times* over breakfast.

> Life *magazine journalist and photographer Edward 'Eddie' Burnet has been killed while flying over Germany with the US Eighth Air Force.*

The article went on to outline his illustrious career.

'Jeezus, Harry, will you look at that! He survived the Spanish Civil War, Dunkirk, the Blitz, and then he gets killed flying out with *us*. That's gotta be a bad omen.'

Just as Harry was searching through the article to find out more, they were interrupted by the genial figure of Ernie Benik.

'Hey, boys,' he said. 'We gotta ground the *Macey May* for the next forty-eight hours. Get her patched up properly.'

Harry hoped they would take them off operational flights and not expect them to fly in another Fortress. It would be good to know no one was going to die over the next two days.

Holberg called them together that afternoon. 'Good news, boys,' he told them as they all stood beneath the nose of the *Macey May*. 'We all got forty-eight-hour passes!'

You could get to London in two or three hours on the train. The whole crew had been talking about taking a trip there ever since they had arrived at Kirkstead. Harry thought of Tilly, but she worked in the factory during the week and so wouldn't be free to go on their daytrip to Norwich so he would have to wait for another time to invite her out.

They all travelled down on the train from Norwich and were at Liverpool Street station by six o'clock. John had been to London before and knew all about the 'tube' – the underground railway that would get them anywhere in the city centre in a matter of minutes.

First stop was Rainbow Corner – the Red Cross club for American servicemen in Piccadilly. The tube was crowded and it was almost impossible to stick together. As they emerged from the underground at Piccadilly Circus they were overwhelmed by the sheer chaos of the city.

In the autumn twilight the pavements were overflowing with servicemen and women from every imaginable Allied nation. Just walking from the station exit to the club on the corner of Shaftesbury Avenue they heard French, Dutch, Polish and several languages they could only guess at.

Every American serving in Britain, and probably everyone in America, had heard about Rainbow Corner. It was the sort of place the news magazines never tired of running features on. They all knew it never closed, and they all knew it served ice-cold Cokes, and burgers just like they made them at home. Holberg had also told his crew that this was the place where the staff sorted out your London accommodation for you.

So they sat at the bar, eagerly engaging other American servicemen in conversation, and discussing what they wanted to do, while the resident staff made phone calls on their behalf. Corrales and Dalinsky hit it off with a guy in the bar who seemed to know exactly what to see and do around London.

The crew all had different ideas. That especially suited Harry, who had started to feel uncomfortable with Skaggs, who he'd noticed bristling angrily when he saw a black American GI with a white girl. Harry shouldn't have been surprised – Skaggs was always very short with the black servicemen who worked in the kitchens and in the maintenance squads.

By the time their hotel rooms had been booked for the night it was nine o'clock. Harry and John had a place in Bloomsbury, not far from Euston Station. They were given a map and instructions to be there for eleven thirty at the latest.

Corrales and Dalinsky had decided they wanted to go to a burlesque show. Skaggs tagged along. Harry saw them disappearing from the bar, their new friend promising they'd 'see more ass than a toilet seat'.

Holberg and his lieutenants decided to visit Covent Garden Opera House – converted into a nightclub for officers 'for the duration'.

John and Harry had simpler pleasures in mind: a meal and a nice old-fashioned London pub.

By the time they left the Rainbow Club it was properly dark and the blackout was still very much enforced. It was disconcerting being in the middle of a mad mass of milling people, all intent on having the time of their life.

On the busy roads buses and taxis crawled through near gridlock, thin beams peeping from covered headlights. Above the buildings, searchlights still criss-crossed the sky, and they had been out in the street for barely a minute when the air-raid sirens began to wail.

So did John. 'Just our luck,' he cried with genuine despair. 'A frigging air raid.'

But no one took a bit of notice. Even when nearby anti-aircraft guns started up, everyone just ignored them. 'When in Rome . . .' said Harry, and continued on, swept up in the crowd.

They found a restaurant barely a minute or two from the Rainbow Club – Lyons Corner House Brasserie, close to Leicester Square – and ate 'fish and chips' which, they had been assured, was a British delicacy. The battered fish was tasteless and nothing like the fish fried in matzah meal that his mom cooked for him back home. John whispered it was probably whale. Harry liked ketchup with his fries, but that was not available. He had to make do with salt and vinegar, which he thought was pretty unpalatable. In fact he wouldn't have eaten his chips if he hadn't been so hungry. The poor quality of the food made Harry feel homesick and he wished he was in a Brooklyn cafe eating salt beef on rye with mustard.

They left the restaurant to wander the streets. Even in the moonlight Harry could make out the great landmarks he'd seen in films and books, like Piccadilly Circus and Regent's Street. But bomb damage was everywhere. Whole blocks had been levelled in the Blitz.

'Hey, John, just think, this is what we're doing to the Krauts,' he said. But even as the words left his mouth he didn't know whether it was a statement of grim revenge or an admission of guilt.

They found a pub easily enough. The centre of London had hundreds of them, and they ended up in one they really liked, just off Oxford Street, called the Pillars of Hercules. Inside its cosy bar they mixed with scores of people from all over the world – US servicemen, Free French soldiers, and plenty of locals all happy to talk. Drinking with a British airman from London, they discovered they were paid at least four times as much as he was. When it was time to go, John offered to buy him a couple of pints 'to keep him going'. The man looked offended, rather than grateful, and John and Harry left in a hurry, sensing things could turn nasty.

They walked back towards their hotel in Bloomsbury, arms around each other's shoulders, singing Al Dexter's 'Pistol Packin' Mama'. A couple of girls wearing bright red lipstick approached them in the street, taking their arms, and asked if they were going their way.

'Come and have some fun with us,' the girls chimed.

John shook the girl off his arm. 'Ladies, thank you, but no thank you,' he said stiffly.

The girls tried to cajole them into going with them but left with a surly, 'Spoilsports, keep your Yankee money to yourselves then,' when they realised they were getting nowhere.

'Let's have one for the road,' said John after they had disappeared. There was a small corner pub called the George, which was almost empty. Like the Pillars of Hercules it was dimly lit, with a coal fire burning in the corner, the flames glinting on the glass and mirrors of the bar.

They sat in the corner, nursing a couple more pints. Harry had never drunk so much in his life and was feeling in a wonderfully good mood. John showed him a picture of his girlfriend, Shirley, taken on the day John had asked her to marry him. She was a pretty girl with curly dark hair. There she was, sitting on a beach somewhere on Long Island, holding her hat as a brisk wind swept over, looking really happy.

John put the photo away, and smiled at Harry fondly and told him he was really glad they'd ended up in the same bomber crew and that he felt like his elder brother.

'I had an elder brother once, but he died,' said Harry, surprising himself. He had never talked about David to any of the guys.

John waited in the pause that followed, weighing up what to say. 'No, kidding,' he replied eventually. 'I had a younger brother once, but he died in the 1937 polio outbreak.'

The coincidence made Harry feel braver and he told John about what had happened with David, and how they had been out in Manhattan when the symptoms first began to show, and he had insisted they stay out there and visit the museum.

John listened intently and when the story was over he put an arm round Harry.

'My cousin's a medic, Harry. He told me, once you've got polio there's nothing medical science can do. They give you medicine that might ease your pain, but no one knows why some people die and some people don't. It wasn't your fault he died.'

Harry had kept these feelings to himself for so long, it felt a relief to have finally shared them with someone. That night he slept better than he had done for years.

The following day they did all the things tourists in London were expected to do – Houses of Parliament, Buckingham Palace, Tower Bridge, St Paul's Cathedral – and caught a train back to Norwich at three in the afternoon. When they returned to Kirkstead there was a note on Harry's bunk: *Come and see me when you get back in, Ernie.*

'Know what this is about?' he asked John.

'No, but I got the same note too. Let's go.'

They sauntered over to the hardstand, bumping into Corrales. 'Had a good time?' asked John. Corrales laughed. 'Better than Skaggs. He got taken into the cells for picking a fight with a black guy with an English girl on his arm.'

'What, he's still locked up?' asked Harry.

'Nah, he came back with me. Dumb redneck. He knows how to mess up a good time. I shoulda made him go with you guys.'

As they approached the *Macey May*'s hardstand John said, 'Maybe we've got more time off? Maybe Ernie's taking longer than he oughta?'

Benik and his crew were still all over the *Macey May* and scaffolding covered the right wing.

Ernie whooped when he saw him. 'Are you boys lucky sons of bitches,' he said. 'Look what we found in the fuel tank!'

He clambered down from the wing and went over to the ground crew utility truck. 'Look at this lot.' Ernie held out three hefty projectiles that covered the entire palm of his left hand.

John whistled. 'Some bullets,' he said.

'They're cannon shells, Hill, not bullets,' said Ernie. 'These things explode on contact. You wouldn't have stood a chance if they'd done what they were supposed to. If they did, your wing would have gone up like a dry hay barn.'

'And why didn't that happen?' asked Harry.

Ernie grinned. 'I opened up one of the shells and found this.' He held out a small crumpled piece of paper. It had been folded meticulously, and scrawled on it in pencil were the words:

Greetings to the brave Allies. This is for you!
From the slave labourers of Essen.

Harry was baffled. Benik could see it in his face. He explained.

'Some guy in the armaments factory, someone the Nazis are forcing to work there, this is his way of getting back at the bastards! He doesn't pack those cannon shells with the explosives that're supposed to go in them. They're duds.'

'You mean if those things went off in the fuel tank . . .' Harry stopped to take in the implications.

Ernie Benik finished his sentence for him. 'Coulda blown the wing off. Or at least set off a big fire. You boys have had a hell of a narrow escape.'

Harry thought about those cannon shells as he lay in his bunk, waiting for sleep to come. He wondered too if the guy who had written that message was Jewish like him. What he had done took guts. Harry's stomach tightened when he thought what the Nazis would do to the worker if they caught him.

* * *

Several days passed and they were all wondering when they would get the next early morning call, but Ernie dropped no hints, they heard no other rumours and no missions were flown. Then the weather had changed. Deep low pressure over most of northern Europe, so the weather boys told them. When the clouds were this thick, nobody did any flying.

Yom Kippur, the Jewish Day of Atonement, came on October 9th, and Bortz asked Harry if he wanted to come to the service they were having in the base chapel, a small hut used by all faiths at Kirkstead. Harry thanked the lieutenant, and was in two minds about going, but he hadn't been to a Jewish service since he was ten and he made his excuses.

On that day it rained until the ground turned to sludge and you couldn't go out the hut without coming back with mud squelching in your shoes and halfway up your trousers. But there were occasional gaps in the rain and they could apply for day passes if they wanted. Harry thought this was a good moment to ask Tilly to take him to Norwich.

He left a note at her grandmother's and she wrote him a letter telling him to meet her at the bus stop on Sunday, nine o'clock sharp, raining or not.

That was the next day. Harry prayed he wouldn't wake up to a blue sky and all leave cancelled due to the imminent recommencement of operations. But his luck held with the weather and he walked down to Kirkstead in a thin drizzle, the cloud as low and grey as ever. Tilly was waiting for him, dressed in a dull brown winter coat, and gave him a dazzling smile when she saw him.

The bus was late but, having both recently returned from London, they had plenty to talk about. They got to Norwich by ten, when the weather took a turn for the worse. Sheltering from the rain they sat together in a half-empty cafe. Tilly took off her overcoat, and shook her hair free of her red beret. She was wearing a Fair Isle cardigan over a green cotton dress and looked so pretty it took his breath away.

As the rain came on stronger the cafe filled up, and they had to squeeze up against each other on a row of benches that leaned against the wall. She didn't seem to mind. One of the things he noticed about her was a faint aroma of woodsmoke – lots of Limeys smelt like that, or of paraffin oil. It wasn't unpleasant.

'Do you have a wood fire at home?' he asked, in an awkward attempt to make conversation.

She laughed. 'We spend most evenings sitting right on top of that fire. There's so little fuel to heat the house, you have to make the most of what you've got.'

She asked him what he wanted to do and suggested they visit the cathedral. 'Just the thing for a rainy day,' she said.

Tilly had been there many times before and pointed out all the things he would have missed if he'd just been wandering around on his own – the quaint little carvings under the seats in the ornate wooden choir, the extraordinary elaborate stonework of the vaulted ceiling in the nave, the stone gargoyles leering from corners, like malevolent creatures in a Walt Disney movie.

The choir began rehearsing for a wedding, and as they sang their voices hung in the air, falling to silence like a great silk veil in the vastness of the nave.

Then, for a brief moment, the sun came out and they went to sit in the cloistered garden. There was no one else around the cloister and Tilly quietly slipped her hand into his. It felt like a last gasp of summer and Harry wished, more than anything else in the world, that he could stop time and stay in this peaceful place forever.

They got back to Kirkstead as evening was falling, and Harry was delighted when she took his arm and asked him to walk her to her grandmother's house. He thought she might ask him in, but instead she said he ought to hurry back to his base as another torrential downpour was imminent. Then she kissed him on the cheek at the garden gate and told him to let her know as soon as he could come and see her again.

Harry was lost for words, and walked back to the base kicking himself for not asking her if she would like to come to the dance they were having at the base mid-month, with a full dance band and everything. He would just have to drop her another note.

CHAPTER 17

October 14th, 1943

Harry was dreaming about his brother. He and David were walking home along the Brooklyn Bridge from Manhattan on a brilliant summer day, a cool breeze from the East River taking some of the heat off. It was the year they built the World Fair in Queens and you could see some of its amazing buildings out there in the distance. It seemed like the most exciting place in the world and they were both going to go as soon as the crowds died down ... Then Harry remembered something he had been dying to tell David for months. 'We went to this jumble sale – that's Limey speak for yard sale – and this duchessy old woman was judging the cake competition ...'

But he realised, even in his dream, that David was dead and this hadn't happened to him yet. He woke to a shaking sensation. It was Ernie Benik. 'Hey, Harry – some dream you were having.' Ernie was smiling. 'I brought you a coffee. You guys have to be up for a briefing.'

Harry came to his senses. John and Ralph were already up, and Ernie was shaking Jim Corrales from a deep slumber. 'Hey, John, what's happening?' called Harry.

'Dunno, buddy,' he said. 'Gotta be an op.'

Within half an hour they were all sitting in the Operations Briefing Room, knocking back black coffee and coughing in the haze of cigarette smoke. Colonel Kittering came in with his entourage of senior officers and the whole room fell silent and stood to attention. The colonel looked immaculate, which surprised Harry as he guessed he had been up all night.

'OK, stand easy,' said Kittering. 'Today the Eighth is going to make history.'

'I don't like the sound of this already,' whispered Corrales.

'Three months back we visited Schweinfurt and Regensburg. Our mission then was to take out the ball-bearing works. I don't need to tell you the whole Nazi war machine depends on these little things. Well, we didn't do as good a job as we could have, and today we're going to finish it off.'

A low groan started in the front rows and spread to the rear as the whole room realised what their target would be.

Kittering drew back the curtain over the map and they all saw a thin red twine stretching from Kirkstead to Schweinfurt, right in the heart of Germany.

Harry wondered if there'd ever been an op where the crew cheered when they saw their destination.

'It's not going to be easy,' said Kittering. 'But I know you can do it. We're sending over three hundred Fortresses, and by early afternoon we're going to have wiped out the Nazi ball-bearing industry. And the history books will say, this was the moment the war started to grind to a halt.'

Harry remembered his first day at Kirkstead, when they had watched the mauled bomb group return from Schweinfurt and had seen that Fortress crash, and was filled with a sense of foreboding. He tried to cheer himself up. Today was a Thursday and on Saturday he was going to the base dance with the most beautiful girl in England. Tilly had written back to his note immediately but told him she could not see him until then, as she was travelling down to London to stay with her mother. She signed off her letter with three kisses. The anticipation had been killing him, but Saturday was now just another 'maybe' too.

When their jeep arrived at the *Macey May*, Holberg was looking worried. He sniffed the air. 'Look at the fields, boys,' he said, staring beyond the wire boundary of the base. 'That's a fog rising. We're not due off for another half-hour so I reckon it'll be all over us by then.'

Harry looked at the wheels of the *Macey May* – the tyres were compressed under the weight of her full fuel tanks and bomb load. Sending heavily loaded bombers off in that fog would be just as dangerous as flying over their target. Surely Kittering and the top brass didn't think so lightly of their lives and their precious aircraft that they'd do such a thing?

'Not looking good,' said Holberg. 'Maybe they won't send us.'

Harry was aware of a sensation he rarely felt these days. Intense relief. If there was fog, how were they going to take off? It would be suicide surely.

'So, Captain, whadda we gonna do?' asked Corrales.

'Better go through the motions, I suppose,' said Holberg.

They grouped together for their ritual moment of prayer. Despite his own dim faith, Harry prayed fervently that they would all make it back.

'OK,' said Holberg, slapping each man on the back. 'Pay attention up there, look out for each other, and tonight I'll be buying you all a beer in the Green Man!'

With that they dispersed to their stations in the Fortress and began the checks that made up the preflight routine.

Harry always found this one of the most nerve-racking times on a mission. Holberg and Stearley had the most to do, checking the engines and all the other vital systems on the bomber, along with LaFitte the engineer. Once Harry had loaded his guns inside his turret and gone through the basic gunsight, oxygen, communications and suit checks, there was nothing else for him to do. Most importantly, there was nothing to distract him from what lay ahead. He sat there in his seat next to Skaggs in the radio op compartment trying to find something interesting in the *Eastern Daily Press* – a dull read at the best of times.

'Hey, Skaggs, says here Elsie Ruddock's won the marrow growing contest, against fierce competition from the Saxmunden WI.'

'What the hell's a marrow?' said Skaggs, barely able to keep the contempt from his voice.

Harry lifted the paper to show him the picture – an ample English matron in her gardening overalls, proudly holding up an equally ample vegetable of some sort. It looked like an elongated pumpkin.

Skaggs lolled back in his chair and let out an almighty snort. 'Never mind that. I wanna know about the Mayor of Beccles and his garden gnomes.'

Harry had noticed some Limeys liked to decorate their gardens with ceramic figures, like those little guys in Snow White. It was one of the baffling things about being in England. Recently the mayor had had three gnomes stolen from his garden. This had made the front page of the paper.

'Maybe some of the guys wanted a souvenir,' sniggered Skaggs.

They settled into a bored silence. Occasionally Harry looked out of the small observation window by Skaggs's desk. 'Fog still rising,' he'd say, and Skaggs would grunt. At any moment, he was sure, a flare would go up instructing them to stand down and they'd all head back to their huts.

But after half an hour the radio transmitter took an incoming message. Skaggs adjusted his interphone and said, 'Radio to Captain. Start engines.'

149

Harry's stomach tightened. They were going after all.

Skaggs saw his concern. He peered out of the large skylight window above his desk. 'No way can we take off in this,' he said to Harry. 'We'll collide with each other on the concrete.'

The *Macey May* started to shudder as each engine burst into life and soon the noise of scores of aero-engines from other bombers nearby made conversation all but impossible. Harry wouldn't have been surprised if you could hear this racket in Norwich. He was sure the girls in Tilly's factory could hear it, and he wondered if she had told any of her friends she was going to the dance with him on Saturday.

His wristwatch crawled through another fifteen minutes. He began to fret too about their fuel supply. The longer they sat there on the concrete, engines running, the less fuel they'd have left to get them safely home.

He went over to Hill and Dalinsky in the waist and peered out of their wide gun port windows. 'Betcha ten dollars we don't go!' said Dalinsky.

Harry shook his head.

'Fog's still thick on the ground,' John said to them both.

Then Dalinsky pointed to a signal flare arcing up from where they knew the control tower was. But this wasn't to tell them to disembark.

'Shit. That's it. We're definitely going,' said Hill.

Dalinsky gave Harry a slap on the back. 'Shoulda made that bet.'

* * *

'OK, strap yourselves in,' said Holberg over the interphone. 'We're off.'

The tone of the *Macey May*'s engines moved up a notch. Harry wished he was there in the cockpit. Holberg had let him stand behind them on one of the early training flights they had all made back in the States, and it was fascinating seeing what those three guys had to do to get a B-17 into the air.

They lurched and dawdled from their hardstand, joining the queue of Fortresses waiting their turn on the main runway. Not knowing what was actually happening made things far worse for Harry. The rest of them could see out of a window. He was just stuck there inside the radio compartment with the *Eastern Daily Press*.

Harry thought he sensed a flash of light, then a low muffled explosion rolled across the base, barely audible over the roar of aero-engines. 'Oh Jesus . . .' he heard Holberg say over the interphone.

'One down, or maybe two,' said Skaggs. 'Maybe there was a collision.'

The *Macey May* trundled forward. Whatever had happened, it hadn't happened on the runway. They were still going.

Holberg's voice crackled in their ears. 'Hold tight!'

The *Macey May* picked up speed, her own engines screaming over the background thrum of all the others. Harry hated this bit. The wait until the bumping stopped and the wheels were clear of the concrete. That awful pause as they climbed, fearing that any second they might plunge to the ground to be consumed by a fiery explosion. Harry often wondered if you died right away when that happened or whether you had to endure an agonising few seconds as the flames ate into you.

They quickly cleared the fog, and after a minute or two the Fortress levelled off and began to circle. This part of the mission was always tense and Harry admired the cool way Holberg and Stearley managed to ease their bomber into the complex combat box formation that was supposed to offer the best protection from Nazi fighters.

'OK, Friedman. Down you go,' said Holberg. Harry unplugged his interphone and Dalinsky and Hill came to help him wriggle into his turret.

'We'll see you over Schweinfurt,' said John.

Harry peered around 360 degrees. Fortresses filled the sky – too many to count. They were halfway down the top box of the combat formation. That was fine. It was the guys at the top and bottom who were always supposed to be most vulnerable, but Harry thought that was bull. He figured blind luck was the only thing that protected you up here.

Skaggs patched in the BBC Home Service. They'd have the music until they were halfway across the Channel. That was a good hour away. Schweinfurt was a long haul, down south over England rather than out east over the North Sea.

Harry continued to make regular sweeps round the whole panorama of the sky as the formation rose to its operational height.

'Oxygen on,' came the command from the cockpit as they passed ten thousand feet. Harry shivered and double-checked his heated suit was plugged in. It was easy to forget these things, or accidentally detach the switches and plugs that kept you alive at twenty-five thousand feet.

That was it for now. The next hour would be eye strain and just those regular ten-minute checks from Holberg or Stearley, making sure their oxygen supply was functioning properly and they were still all conscious. He wished Holberg allowed them to chat at this stage of the mission, just idle banter to make him feel less isolated, but the captain was very strict on that point. Only operational talk was permitted. It was the only way to make sure they all came back alive, he told them. Harry knew other crews chatted because they'd told him, but he liked Holberg too much to argue the point with him.

They were supposed to meet up with their fighter escort just as they reached the outer fringes of London. The Thunderbolt and Lightning fighter planes would be flying with them until they reached the limits of their range.

'Can't see those fighters,' said Harry over the interphone. 'Anyone else spot 'em?'

'Bad news, boys.' Holberg sounded matter-of-fact. 'We heard from control that the fighters missed the rendezvous because we were so late taking off.'

There was a chorus of disappointed moans and even some swearing.

'What a screw-up,' spat Corrales. 'Why didn't they tell them to wait? Take off a bit later?'

'Ours is not to question why,' said Holberg. 'But you've got to be extra vigilant now. Expect Fritz to come down on us any time over the Channel.'

The bomb group thundered south-east, but all of the *Macey May*'s crew were disconcerted to see a steady stream of bombers leaving their combat boxes and heading for home. No one said anything, until Holberg spoke, his scepticism clear in his voice. 'What the hell? There can't be that many mechanical failures in just one mission.'

That was an excuse for all the crew to voice their resentments.

'Captain, I gotta broken nail.'

'My coffee's gone cold in my thermos – we gotta go back.'

'Hey, guys, I got something in my eye. Can't we turn back, please?'

'All right, guys, keep it down,' said Holberg. 'I'm going to have to tighten up our formation here. Keep your eyes open and let me know if we get too close to our buddies.'

It was alarming flying these tight formations. You could see the men in the other planes, as they sat in the cockpit or at the waist firing positions. Harry wished they could move a little further away. He could see how easy it would be for a panicked gunner to fire an accidental stream of bullets into one of their own planes, and how dangerous it would be for the adjacent aircraft if one of them had a direct hit from flak.

Despite the grey sky Harry could see the landmarks of London, tiny from this great height but just about recognisable. There was that big loop in the river not long past Tower Bridge. He remembered seeing a great formation pass over high in the sky when he was there a few days before, little silver specks with long vapour trails. The kids on the sidewalks had all pointed. He wondered too what the Luftwaffe used to think as they came over to destroy this great city during the Blitz a couple of years before. So far, the Eighth Air Force had only been asked to bomb industrial targets. He'd heard the Brits dropped tons of bombs on big cities, the only way they could be sure to hit anything important in the dark. They called it carpet-bombing. He didn't like the sound of that. He accepted that sometimes civilians would be killed by American bombs, but he didn't know how he would feel if they sent them to carpet-bomb those big civilian centres.

They left the landmarks of London behind and the Channel came into view. Then they headed out over the open sea.

'OK, Skaggs, let's have that radio off,' said Holberg.

Within minutes they would be in range of enemy fighters, and once again their lives would be dangling by a slender silver thread.

CHAPTER 18

The *Macey May* was half an hour over France when they came.

'Eleven o'clock high.' The voice was Bortz's. 'Right on the edge of vision. There's hundreds of them.'

'OK. Thank you, Lieutenant,' said Holberg. 'They're just getting in position so they can come down out of the sun, so expect them any minute . . .'

The German fighters always did this – dived down with the sun right behind them, so it was difficult to see them coming without dazzling yourself.

The next thing Harry heard froze his blood. 'What the hell is this?' It was Bortz again.

Cain had got up from his seat at the navigator's table in the nose, to peer through the Plexiglas cone. 'There's trails of smoke coming towards us at speed,' he told them all. Then his voice quickened. 'I'd guess they're rockets.'

In a flash a rocket passed by the *Macey May*'s right wing and continued through the formation. There was a flash, and a grotesque boiling cloud of flame formed a few hundred feet below. Harry could see it all in his turret.

'Fortress hit, four o' clock low,' he reported. One second it was there, the next the whole plane was a mass of fire and flying fragments.

There were further explosions around them and the *Macey May* bucked in the sky.

'Oh God,' said Dalinsky. 'The whole wing's gone.'

Harry immediately swung his turret round. Their wings were fine. Dalinsky had been talking about another Fortress. He saw it a moment later, nose down and dropping like a brick below them. He couldn't imagine anyone getting out of that. The whole right wing was ablaze and falling behind the rest of the bomber.

Holberg came on. 'Here they come. Don't waste your ammo. Fire within range and watch out for ours.'

Then Stearley spoke. 'They only hit two with those rockets.' That was something to hold on to.

All at once the sky was full of targets. It was difficult to hit anything that sped past faster than the human eye could track it. It was like hurtling through a train station at speed and trying to read its name on the platform signs – almost impossible.

On that first pass Harry barely fired his guns. But when the Messerschmitts and Focke-Wulfs came back for a second time, his job was easier. All around now, he could hear or sense the crew firing their weapons. Down to the left he noticed a Focke-Wulf lining up for a shot at the bomber beneath them.

Harry waited for the fighter to fly level, then he let off a long stream of bullets. He could see shards of metal dance along the top of the fuselage and the cockpit canopy shattered. He knew in an instant he must have killed the pilot. Flames burst out from the engine and the plane started to dive, trailing a thick plume of flame and smoke.

'Got one,' he said, trying to suppress his excitement. This was his first certain hit. He was surprised at how little he cared that he had just killed a young pilot.

German fighters continued to buzz around them like angry hornets. Then, in an instant, they were gone. Harry rotated his turret straight ahead. The reason was plain enough. A mile or so in front of them was a dense field of flak. No sooner had one ordeal ended than another began.

The *Macey May* started to jolt and jerk around. Harry felt sick and simultaneously hot and cold. Inside his flying suit he was bathed in sweat.

Holberg had had a change of mind about when Harry should come out of his turret. Now it was only when they were over the target. Flak was usually at its worst then, but he should stay put at all other times apart from take-off and landing.

'It's looking clear up ahead,' Holberg told them. 'Another minute of this and we're through. Hold tight.'

Hold tight. Every part of Harry was scrunched up tight. His fists, his eyes, his toes . . . This was the worst flak he had ever been in. Flak burst close to the *Macey May* and he could hear its shrapnel shards whine around. Some struck the plane with a dull thump. He didn't worry too much about that. Everyone seemed to come back from Germany with holes in the fuselage or the wings.

The flak died down and all of a sudden they were riding through clear air, plain sailing in level flight, the patchwork fields of occupied Europe stretching beneath them.

'Schweinfurt ETA ten minutes,' said Cain.

Holberg came on. 'Let's make sure you're all here.' He ran through the crew.

No fighters appeared in the last interminable ten minutes, and as they approached the target, Holberg told Harry he could come out from his turret as soon as the flak started to burst around the plane. It was inevitable, of course, that there was flak around a target. It wouldn't be worth attacking if there wasn't flak.

The first bursts of explosives started to bloom around the combat box like dirty flower heads. Harry was all set to go when he heard something over his headphones that turned him cold with fear.

'Bortz, do you copy?' said the captain. 'Are you set to take over?'

The flak was getting worse by the minute.

Bortz did not respond. Holberg asked again, more urgently.

There was still no response.

'Cain, can you hear me?' said the captain. 'What's happening with Bortz?'

There was no reply and Harry felt in desperate need of water. His mouth was bone dry.

Then Cain came on. 'Bortz is OK. I'll speak to him directly.'

Harry breathed again.

There was another pause.

'His headset's not working.'

'Lieutenant, get Bortz up here,' Holberg said. 'Bombardier's got to have a headset.'

Then Harry heard him say, 'Go to the midsection and see if there's a spare with Skaggs. If he can't help, then take one off Hill or Dalinsky.'

Harry had heard enough. He unplugged himself and set up the complex mechanism to get himself out of the turret.

Harry got to the radio compartment just as Bortz burst through the other door. They both saw Skaggs at once. He was slumped face forward and they thought him asleep, or maybe passed out from a faulty oxygen mask. Bortz shook him, but he remained inert.

The Fortress jolted in the air as flak exploded nearby and Skaggs slid brusquely off his chair to lie face up on the floor. His eyes stared into nothing. He was dead.

Bortz and Harry picked him up and propped him against the side of the fuselage. As they did so, Bortz pointed to a small cut in Skaggs's windpipe. As he slumped forward exposing the back of his neck they saw the entry wound. A bullet or a piece of flak had gone through a vertebra in his neck. It must have killed him in an instant.

160

Bortz plugged his interphone cord into the compartment jack box. 'Captain, Skaggs is dead,' he said. There was no reply.

They hauled Skaggs back on his chair, holding him in place with the seat straps. Thank God it was a clean death, Harry thought.

'Gotta have one of these,' said Bortz, and carefully detached Skaggs's headset from his lolling head. 'Jesus, it's warm.' He shuddered.

Then he was gone, back to the front of the plane.

'Right. Target five minutes,' said Holberg. 'Bortz, handing over to you.'

Harry strapped himself into his seat in Skaggs's compartment. It was awful sitting there with a dead man. Skaggs's mouth was hanging open and sightless eyes were staring at the ceiling. Sometimes Harry had found it hard to like him, but he was still his buddy, and now he was gone he felt a terrible sadness.

The flak was really intense now, and Harry wondered whether to just sit tight or watch out of the top window of the radio compartment. He decided his best bet was to curl up into a ball and listen to Bortz going through his bomb-aiming routine. 'Two minutes . . . Target in sight . . .'

Immediately to his side Skaggs flinched and jerked upright. Harry nearly jumped out of his skin. Another piece of flak had pierced the plane and hit the radio operator right in the middle of his forehead. Skaggs was dead twice over. If his first injury hadn't broken his neck, the second one would have gone straight through his brain. Harry began to shake uncontrollably and was grateful no one else was around to see him. He fought back tears of sheer terror and began to pray under his breath.

Over the interphone Bortz sounded icy calm. 'Steady, Thirty seconds . . .' That brought Harry back to earth.

Flak continued to burst all around the ship, and when Harry dared to look from the small window in the operator's compartment, he was amazed that anyone and anything could fly through it and survive. At four o'clock low there was another Fortress going down in a ball of flame. At any second that could be them. Harry bit his lip hard and tried not to think about it.

All at once the *Macey May* lifted in the air and Holberg came over the interphone.

'Job done. Let's go home.' The Fortress banked sharply to the west and once again the flak disappeared from the sky.

'Harry, back to your turret,' said Holberg, but Harry never heard him; he was already halfway there, stopping for a brief second to pat Hill and Dalinsky on the shoulder.

Ten minutes away from Schweinfurt Harry's headphone crackled. This time it was John Hill. 'Think I see them coming out the sun.'

The sun had moved round in the sky so this time they were side on: good news for the bombardier and pilots and all the other guys at the front of the aircraft – not so good for the rest of the crew.

'Definite. Three o'clock high,' shouted John.

Again the German fighters swarmed around them. Harry thought he heard Dalinsky cheering, and a moment later he saw a Messerschmitt plummet down in a steep dive, thick black smoke spewing from its engine. The canopy flew off and a tiny figure tumbled from the cockpit, his parachute opening a moment later. Mesmerised by the sight, Harry forgot to keep sweeping through his constant circles.

'Hey, Friedman, Focke seven o'clock low,' said Corrales. 'Let's nail him.'

As the turret swept round, he could see the unmistakable outline of the Focke-Wulf closing fast. It was right in his sight and as Harry began to fire he also saw four distinct flashes in the nose and inner wing of the approaching fighter. A second later the Focke began to trail black smoke and it veered off sharply to the left. Harry continued to fire into the plunging fighter watching his bullets spatter along the length of the fuselage.

But Harry and Corrales had fired a moment too late. Under the plane, Harry noticed a line of black smoke trailing away from the *Macey May*. When he turned his turret he could see the outer engine on the left side was on fire. Seconds later Holberg's voice crackled in the interphone. 'Cut number one. Extinguishers on.' The propeller stopped spinning moments later.

'OK, fellas. Keep your eyes on the sky. We all still here?' The crew reported back, one by one from the tail of the

Fortress, apart from Skaggs. Harry shivered. It was awful not to hear that Southern drawl in the crew roll call.

The engine had stopped flaming, but an intermittent trail of smoke still seeped from the edge of the wing. Harry noticed with consternation that the *Macey May* was having trouble keeping up with the others in the combat box. A lone Fortress was almost certainly doomed. A sole focus for flak and a sure kill for a fighter *Schwarm* who might happen upon it. The *Carolina Peach* boys certainly never made it back.

'Flak ahead,' said Bortz.

A minute later the Fortress began its shaking and lurching as the sky filled up with dense black puffs of smoke. The familiar terror returned.

'Clear ahead,' said Bortz.

There was a sudden rattle of machine-gun fire and Harry instinctively spun his turret through 360 degrees searching for fighters. Surely they wouldn't attack here? 'What's happening?' he heard himself say over the interphone. Firing seemed to be coming from inside the plane, right above his head. 'Where are they?' he said again. Not being able to even see his attacker, especially one this close, was more frightening than having them swarm around you.

'Friedman, keep it quiet,' said Holberg, and rattled through the crew. John Hill, Ralph Dalinsky and Jim Corrales did not reply.

Harry felt sick with worry and asked Holberg if he could get out into the waist and help with any injuries.

'No. Stay at your station. Stearley, go and find out what's happening.'

Another few shots rattled off above. Almost like fire crackers. Maybe one of the gunners had spotted something. Then a sharp whine made him flinch. A bullet had pierced the thin metal skin of his turret, just above his head. He immediately turned around 360 degrees, scanning the sky for enemy fighters, but he couldn't see any.

Harry breathed deeply, trying to stop himself shaking after his near miss. He had to wait an age, wondering what had happened and who was alive and who was dead or injured, before Holberg's voice crackled in his ear.

'OK. We have casualties. Hill's down and Corrales. Stearley's patching them up. Friedman, you've got to work extra hard. Dalinsky's OK but his gun mount is damaged.' Then he said, 'Harry – you did a great job on the Focke-Wulf. We'll be OK as long as you keep your wits about you. Flak's gone. I can't see any in front of us. So the fighters will be back soon enough.'

By now the *Macey May* was noticeably lagging behind the other Fortresses. Her three remaining engines were screaming to keep up, but even the loss of a few miles an hour soon showed in a bomber formation.

They were at the tail end of the formation now. Still protected by the guns of the other Fortresses, but an obvious target for a fighter looking for an easy kill.

A smattering of flak burst around them as they passed over Dortmund. It came and went so quickly no one thought to mention it, but soon after it stopped Harry was alarmed to notice another trail of smoke – this time on the right wing outer engine.

'Captain, there's another engine on fire,' he said.

Holberg came back over the interphone. 'Yeah, we know. LaFitte's shutting it down.'

The prop stopped revolving but the smoke carried on pouring out, with an occasional burst of flame. There was a lot of fuel in the wing tanks. If that caught, things could turn nasty pretty quickly.

Harry began to feel horribly claustrophobic in his little turret. The outer left engine had stopped smoking now, but this one on the other wing was a crisis that could turn into a catastrophe. He watched that engine far more than he watched the skies. The fire seemed to be spreading.

If it reached the inner engine or started to burn along the whole wing then the Fortress would drop like a stone.

'Captain, you want me to stay put?' Harry couldn't help asking. 'Maybe John could do with some help.'

Holberg was stern. 'Friedman, we've got it under control. If we're going to bail out, you'll see that red light. Until then you keep at your station.'

Harry burned with shame. He knew asking to leave his turret was strictly against flying regulations. The whole crew would have heard his request. He realised more than ever how important it was not to let them down.

The loss of the second engine made everything far more dangerous. Now the *Macey May* was a definite straggler. She was losing height too – just below the lowest level of the combat box and maybe a third of a mile behind. But the ground was still a long way down. They had bombed at thirty thousand feet – the limit of their capacity. Now they were probably at twenty-five thousand.

'Here come the fighters,' said Cain, in the nose.

Harry scanned the sky. Now the *Macey May* was below the bomber formations he could see very little, and none of the other guys were firing or warning of incoming fighters.

Holberg let the crew at the back know what was happening. 'They're leaving us alone. Maybe they think we're not worth the bother.'

Almost simultaneously, Harry could see two flaming B-17s about half a mile in front of them, plunging to the ground. One exploded during its dive, debris tumbling earthward in great flaming chunks, a wing spinning over and over. The other carried on in its relentless trajectory, sure to hit the ground far sooner. There was another smaller shape falling too, obscured by its own flaming plume. That must be a fighter plane.

Dalinsky called over the interphone 'Four o'clock level, Messerschmitt.'

Harry spun round but he could see nothing. Dalinsky was obviously working both those waist guns. With a sickening feeling Harry wondered what had happened to John. Was he still alive?

'Can't see him, probably coming up behind us,' said Dalinsky.

Holberg called out, anxiety plain in his voice. 'Dalinsky, get down to the tail gun.'

A few seconds later, Dalinsky's voice crackled over the interphone. 'Captain, Corrales is all over it.'

Harry wasn't quite sure what Dalinsky meant by that, but he could guess. The tail gunner must have been caught by a hail of cannon fire. He thought of Corrales' face, the way he looked when he made a wisecrack; he felt his gut wrench and had to suppress the urge to vomit.

'Damn it, Dalinsky. Get down there, or do I have to go myself?' Holberg was really rattled now.

Then Harry called over. 'He's right on our left flank.'

He was too. Flying exactly parallel with the *Macey May*, close enough to see the pilot's face. For all the world it looked like the German fighter plane was escorting them. It was certainly not a position you adopted if you were about to shoot a bomber down.

Harry thought to shoot, but the Messerschmitt kept bobbing just above his line of fire.

'Hold fire, everyone.' That was Holberg's voice. Harry wondered what on earth had got into him.

Then LaFitte's voice came over the interphone 'He's saluting us.'

'Probably thinks we've had it and we're not worth wasting bullets on.' The relief was palpable in Holberg's voice. 'Well, I reckon he's made a mistake. We've got enough fuel to get back over the Channel, and we're maintaining our height. If nothing else happens, we can do it.'

Hauptmann Heinz Frey's Messerschmitt had flown parallel with the cockpit close enough to see the Fortress's name on its nose – *Macey May II*. To him, the bomber looked mortally wounded. As well as the smoking engines, there were great chunks missing from the fuselage, you could see the supporting struts of the interior, like a skeleton beneath the skin and muscle of an animal, and the rear of the tail was in tatters. The gunner in there couldn't possibly have survived that. Frey could not see the point in wasting any more of his precious bullets. He could even see the faces of the two pilots. They were young men, just like him. He was going to give them a chance, let them parachute to safety. To attack them now would be cold-blooded murder.

Frey banked away and flew south-west until the B-17 was out of sight.

CHAPTER 19

Between the *Macey May* and an uncertain landing at an airbase in the south-east of England lay 250 miles of enemy territory and almost certain annihilation. The outer right engine continued to burn. There was obviously a fuel leak somewhere that couldn't be isolated. Sometimes the flames flared out and started to burn along the wing edge, then they would retreat back to the engine housing. Harry tried to take his eyes off the fire and continued to sweep the sky.

'Flak ahead,' said Bortz. Harry tried not to think about what a sitting duck they were, now the main formation was several miles ahead of them. They would present a single irresistible target to the anti-aircraft gunners on the ground.

A minute later a bust of flak shook the Fortress. But there were no more explosions and Holberg came over the interphone. He sounded jubilant. 'We're still pretty high up. It'll be like finding a needle in a haystack for those flak crews. But keep an eye out for fighters.'

Then something happened to turn Harry's blood to ice.

All around the top of his trousers was stained red. He thought he must have been hit by that flak burst and not even realised it. He went hot and cold, and started to shake. Somehow a bullet had gone through him and he didn't even feel it. Sometimes that happened in combat. He had even heard of gunners losing fingers and not even noticing until afterwards. With another shiver, he wondered when it was going to start to hurt and when he was likely to lose consciousness.

'I'm hit,' he called over the interphone. No one responded.

For a moment he stopped. Maybe if he remained in that fetal position, all hunched up in the ball, he'd be OK. He began to dread the stretching and contortions necessary to get himself out of the turret. They said stomach wounds were the most painful, and that was when he would find out exactly what they meant.

A blood-red blob dripped down above him and landed on his trousers. He looked up. There was a pool of red liquid spreading over the top of the turret. In an instant he realised this was hydraulic fluid – an essential part of the mechanism that made his turret slide around and up and down so gracefully. No wonder he didn't feel any pain. He hadn't been hit at all.

His relief was short-lived. If the hydraulics were leaking, then did the turret still work? He pressed down on the foot pedal. Nothing happened. Almost certainly a projectile had pierced the mechanism.

As he tried to fight down his panic, there was a jolt and a burst of flame. The fire had now spread to occupy the whole wing between both the right engines.

'Captain, the turret has stopped working,' he called.

There was a silence. Had his interphone stopped too? Or maybe Holberg didn't believe him.

Then the captain's voice came over the interphone. 'OK, Friedman. You can come out.'

Harry began frantically turning the levers and cranks that manually operated the turret. Under hydraulic power it operated with swift and smooth efficiency. The cranks and levers were stiff from underuse and they moved the turret in barely discernible increments.

The *Macey May* lurched in the sky and the working right wing engine gave a loud bang, like a car backfiring, and there was a further belch of flame and thick black smoke.

'Oh God, somebody help me,' said Harry under his breath. He was drenched in cold sweat now. The *Macey May* banked to the left, flying ten degrees down from the horizontal. Harry's heart was in his mouth and he prayed that this wasn't the moment Holberg lost control and the Fortress went into a steep terminal dive.

The bomb bay doors sprang open and Harry saw two bodies drop, too fast to see who they were. His red light – the signal to bail out – was still not on. Had two guys at the front decided they were going while they could? Was he the only one left? Had Holberg and Stearley abandoned ship and forgotten to let him know?

172

He kept turning the handle to crank the turret into the straight-down position he needed to open the hatch and get out, but it was getting increasingly difficult. Then he heard banging above his head. There was shouting too. 'Come on, Friedman.' It was Stearley.

The turret stopped and would not move further. It was almost in position but not quite. He was trapped.

'Hey, Friedman, watch your head.' Harry could hear the lieutenant easily enough; with two of the engines down, the noise inside the *Macey May* was not so intense.

The plane lurched again to fly level but then tilted sickeningly to the right. There it stayed. Holberg was obviously having real problems flying level. Harry wondered how much longer he would be able to maintain control.

When the plane steadied, there was a terrible banging right over Harry's head. He tried to curl into a little ball, but there was barely space to change his position as it was. He held his hands over his head, feeling the blows mere inches from his flying helmet. They stopped, and when he looked up he could see Stearley had bashed a dent in the thin aluminium hatch. Now he was levering it open with a large wrench from the toolbox in the radio compartment.

Stearley reached in to help Harry out. The *Macey May* lurched again in the sky and the two of them fell against the side of the plane. It was freezing there with a strong rush of incoming air from the bomb bay doors and great holes scattered around the fuselage.

Harry took a look around the waist. 'Jesus Christ,' he said. Now he could see what had happened earlier. An ammunition box had exploded, adding to the bullet holes that peppered the fuselage. In places the whole fabric of the aircraft had torn away.

Dalinsky was pitched over by the left waist window, his back pressed against the side of the plane. He had a great black stain on his flying jacket, spreading out from the middle of his chest. Even though his oxygen mask was still attached to his face, there was a stillness about him that told Harry he was dead. He must have been caught by that last flak burst.

John was there too, lying on his back. Great patches of blood had seeped through his flying suit and blood was also spreading across the wooden floorboards beneath him. His eyes were screwed tight. He was still alive and obviously in a lot of pain.

Harry took off his own glove and one of John's and held his friend's left hand, choking back a cry of despair.

'Harry,' John said between laboured breaths. 'A favour . . . top pocket . . . there's a photo.'

It was the one of his girl, Shirley, holding on to her hat on the beach. John had shown it to Harry when they were in London and told him he had just asked her to marry him.

John held the picture in his right hand, his face scrunched up in pain, his breath coming in short gasps. Then something left him. The photo flew from his dead hand, caught in the swirling currents that buffeted the inside of the

Fortress, and disappeared through one of the gaping holes close to the tail.

Harry felt John's hand go limp in his. He stood up in a daze, overwhelmed by what was happening around him.

The view down to the tail was obscured by the tail wheel housing, but he could see the rear gun position was heavily damaged, with several large holes open to the sky.

'What happened to Corrales?' he asked Stearley.

The lieutenant just shook his head.

'Is he definitely dead? Don't we need to help him?'

A further shake of the head. Then Stearley said, 'Friedman, get out now, or stay and help us. It's OK if you go. LaFitte and Bortz have already jumped.'

'I'll stay,' said Harry. 'What do you want me to do?'

'We need to see if Cain's still in the nose. Maybe he's injured. Maybe he's gone too. And see what we can do to help Berg . . .' Stearley's words were snatched from his mouth. The *Macey May* gave another lurch from the horizontal. It steadied, still on a ten-degree tilt.

'Get your chute on,' said the co-pilot.

Harry reached for his chute, hanging in the waist above his turret, but it was ripped to pieces, silk spilling out under the radio op table.

'You gotta take Skaggs's chute,' said Stearley.

Between them they managed to lift the radio operator's dead body up from his seat and detach the parachute from his back. Harry realised afresh he had never done a parachute jump before and now he felt horribly unprepared.

The *Macey May* lurched again, forward this time. And began a slight but definite dive.

The dive grew steeper. The two remaining engines were screaming. Another explosion just outside shook the plane, and through the little observation window Harry could see the whole wing was ablaze. Stearley was forcing himself along, battling the inrushing air from the bomb bay and G-forces that were pushing him back like a strong gale.

Harry grabbed the parachute from Stearley's hand and had strapped it on his back just as the *Macey May* began to tip to the right. For a moment he thought Holberg must have regained control of the aircraft but the turn continued and he realised this was a spin rather than a controlled manoeuvre. If they were going to get out, they had mere seconds to do it.

His body was pressed hard against the side of the plane and Harry scrambled desperately to fasten the parachute. As he locked in the final clip the spinning grew intolerable. He was pinned against the side as surely as if he were held by shackles. He could feel the flesh on his face pulling back and his eyes bulged open. Stearley was close by, struggling to extract himself, a look of pure horror on his face.

Through the fuselage Harry could feel the heat of the wing fire on his back – even through the thickness of his flying suit. The heat and smoke were catching in his throat. The bulkhead partition was pressing hard into his shoulder. Would he burn to death in the air or be killed in one final hammer blow as the Fortress plunged to the ground? Harry prayed he would not still be conscious when either of those things came to pass.

There was a horrible shearing sound just behind him and he felt the weight of the plane change. The spinning stopped but he was also aware of the sensation of falling even faster through the sky. The intense heat had gone, but that probably meant the wing had broken away. Any tiny fraction of hope that Holberg would retain control of his doomed bomber was gone. The spinning started again and this time Harry felt his blood begin to drain from his head. There was no doubt now. He was going to die. The last thing he saw before he lost consciousness was Stearley's terrified face.

CHAPTER 20

In the blackness there was a grinding, cranking sound, like the sky being ripped to pieces, and Harry's blood-starved brain told him that was the airplane crashing into the ground. He thought it would be painful but it wasn't at all, and now he was falling through crisp clear air, feeling strangely serene about his own death. He was terrified before it happened of course, but this wasn't too bad.

It was cold though – really cold. He could feel wind whipping past his face, and his hair was going all over the place. Suddenly he opened his eyes. He was falling though the sky, and the ground was rushing towards him at terrifying speed. There was a forest below, and fields and hedges, all close enough to see in some detail.

Groggy though he was, he instinctively reached for the release mechanism on his parachute and the silk canopy slithered out of its bag like a high-speed snake. There was a crack of air as his chute billowed over his head, followed by a sharp pain in his crotch – like being kicked in the nuts. The jerk of the harness left him breathless, as the parachute stalled his fall.

All at once the ground stopped hurtling towards him. There was a field with cows in it and the forest he had seen. Harry decided the field was a better place to land and he would steer towards that. He was momentarily distracted by several violent crashes – like a house collapsing. He supposed that was the *Macey May* hitting the ground somewhere behind him. He realised with sickening certainty that those were the moments anyone left in the B-17 met a violent death.

He turned to see two palls of smoke and flame rising from fields maybe a mile away. Mesmerised by the debris that had once been his Fortress, he hit the ground unexpectedly, with a hefty thud that jarred every bone in his body. He was lucky. It was soft and muddy. The chute came down right on top of him, leaving him struggling to unravel himself.

As he emerged from the tangle of silk and cord, he realised he had just made his first parachute jump. Harry had felt so frightened as he fell through the sky it didn't occur to him that this was an entirely new experience. He felt a momentary relief that he had managed it without breaking a limb.

Harry hoped no one had seen him falling through the sky. He wondered where he was and tried to remember all the things they'd told him in escape classes. Gather your chute and bury it. Make contact with the local Resistance. Get out of your flying clothes as soon as possible. But what was he supposed to do? Walk round in his electrically heated long johns?

He gathered the chute and folded it as best he could, then carried it over his shoulder and dragged his bruised and aching body into the shelter of the trees.

A watery sun peeped out from behind the clouds and Harry stared up through the branches and fading tattered leaves at the sky. He had been up there just minutes before. How had he got out of that airplane? Almost certainly it had broken into pieces on the way down.

He had nearly died several times today. He had survived while many of the crew hadn't. Cain, Holberg, they had still been on board. They must have died in the crash. Did Stearley escape like him? And he knew for sure John Hill, Dalinsky, Corrales and Skaggs were dead. He didn't know whether to feel devastated or ecstatic. He had felt a moment of relief when he hit the ground. Now he just felt dazed and numb.

The sun disappeared behind a cloud and exhaustion swept over him. As his eyelids began to droop he noticed another Fortress through the trees, smoke pouring from two right engines. It was maybe a thousand feet in the air. Had the crew escaped? He could see the bomb bay doors open, so maybe they had all jumped. The aircraft was going to crash somewhere around here, but in truth he didn't care. He was alive. That was all that mattered. This morning, when they had all gathered together in front of the *Macey May* before take-off, seemed like a lifetime ago.

Harry was supposed to bury his parachute, but he knew he might have to sleep outdoors and he was reluctant to get rid of something that would keep him warm at night. So he carried it over his shoulder and walked deeper into the forest. Here he would decide what to do next.

He needed to stop and rest. Absent-mindedly glancing at his wristwatch, he realised he had lost it. It was probably somewhere in the wreckage of the *Macey May*. He came to a dip in the ground, full of fallen leaves. This seemed as good a place as any to hide. So he wrapped himself in the chute, then covered himself with leaves and in seconds he was asleep.

Back at the *Macey May*'s hardstand at Kirkstead, the ground crew were getting increasingly despondent. It was starting to get dark now and the chill autumn wind didn't help; even in the fur-lined flying jackets most had managed to beg or steal over the months, they were chilled to the bone. Four of the squadron's twelve Fortresses had failed to return with the rest, and the last of the stragglers had come in on two engines at least half an hour ago. Ernie Benik glanced at his wristwatch and knew Holberg's Fortress would have run out of fuel long ago. Ernie gathered his crew around. 'Boys, they're not coming back.'

They walked back to their hut. The weight of their loss hung dense and silent, like a great black cloud. Ernie cracked open a bottle of rum and poured them all a drink.

When Harry woke he noticed at once that it was almost dark, and he could see the branches on the trees above him silhouetted against a blue-black sky. All at once he realised he would now be posted missing and his parents would have no idea whether he was alive or dead. The thought troubled him immensely until he was distracted by the distant sound of barking. He wondered if there was a search party with tracker dogs out to find downed Allied airmen.

With the prospect of capture looming he felt in his flying jacket pocket for his copy of the *Eastern Daily Press*. It had gone. Sometime, during this terrible day, he had lost it. He felt around his neck for his dog tags, remembering that American airmen who had lost theirs could be shot as spies. Those tags were still there. But then he remembered with a start that his tags had an 'H' for Hebrew stamped on them. They'd been told the Nazis were supposed to treat Jewish Americans the same as any other soldier or airman. But they'd been told a lot of things and not all of them were true. He wondered if there was anything about his appearance that the Germans might think especially Jewish, and whether this would make him easy to spot.

Harry was warm in his parachute and his flying clothes, but he was also very thirsty and hungry. Reluctantly he stirred himself, folded his parachute and picked his way through the debris of the forest.

After ten minutes he stumbled across a path and, as he could think of no better plan, he followed it. By now it was dark, but a three-quarter moon cast a light that was bright enough to see where he was going.

His thirst was tormenting him now and his tongue was sticking to the roof of his mouth. Ahead he could see a clear horizon between the trees. Here was the edge of the forest. Beyond lay a farmhouse clearing with several surrounding buildings, including a barn. And it was likely the farm would have been built close to a stream or brook.

Harry crept cautiously forward. There was a dim light on in the kitchen, and shadows flitted across the curtains. In escape classes they had warned them that not every French or Dutch civilian would be interested in helping them – indeed, they might immediately betray them.

Harry thought the barn offered him the best place to hide, and when he peered into it, the interior just about discernible in the dim light of the moon, he could see it was a good spot. He also heard two sounds that lifted his spirits: the clucking of hens and the trickle of a brook.

He could wait no longer. Following the sound of running water, Harry went face down on the edge of a small brook, indifferent to the mud on its bank. He drank down the cold, clear water until he could drink no more.

Back at the barn he looked at the hens and wondered if he could eat a raw egg. But with his stomach now full of water, his hunger pangs also subsided. He climbed stacked hay bales to the top of the barn, arranged himself at its far edge and wrapped his parachute around him again.

Sleep was hard to come by, but sometime in the night he dozed off and woke with the sun streaming through the rickety roof. His thirst had returned, and his hunger. There were several hen hutches alongside one of the inner walls of the barn, and there, he was sure, he would find eggs.

It must be fairly early, and Harry supposed if he was quick he might be able to find an egg or two without anyone seeing him.

The hens started clucking as he approached the hutches. He rustled through hay bedding and found what he was looking for – a fresh egg, still slightly warm. Just as he removed it, he heard a small scream and turned to see a girl with a wicker basket just inside the barn. Before he could say anything she had run off, and a moment or two later returned with a man Harry assumed was her father. He had a shotgun, and pointed it straight at him.

Harry put his hands in the air and spoke rapidly. '*Américain! Américain!*'

The man lowered his gun and nodded. '*Attendez,*' he said, and pointed his gun up to the top of the barn. That sounded like French, so Harry supposed France was where he had come down. Meekly making his way back to the spot where he had slept, he did just that – waited.

He toyed with the egg, wondering if he could eat it, and his hunger got the better of him. He'd had uncooked eggs before of course. Eggnog – whipped eggs with milk and sugar – was a Thanksgiving tradition. But a raw egg on its own . . . the idea revolted him. He cracked the egg and emptied both halves into his mouth, swallowing as quickly as he could, and willing it to stay down. The compulsion to retch quickly passed.

Harry was just wondering if he could steal another egg when he heard footsteps. This was the moment when he would discover if someone had come to arrest him or help him.

A gnarled old man in a flat cap, his skin brown and wrinkled, was standing at the entrance of the barn with the man he had seen earlier. They gestured for Harry to climb down.

'*Bonjour, monsieur, je suis un américain,*' he called quietly in his high-school French.

'*Je sais,*' said the man – I know – then he began to jabber incomprehensibly and Harry realised speaking in French had been a bad idea.

He shook his head. '*Pardon, monsieur, je parle seulement un petit peu de français.*'

'*Je sais,*' said the man again.

The two Frenchmen shook hands and then the new arrival grabbed Harry by the arm. '*Venez,*' he said, and led him to a horse and cart piled with the last of the summer's hay. '*Vite, monsieur, cachez-vous ici.*'

His meaning was clear. Hide in here. Harry couldn't believe his luck and burrowed beneath the hay. The cart began to move a moment later. Harry could sense it trundling slowly up a hill, but as they reached the crest and began to head down he could hear voices he recognised as German – soldiers, almost certainly called out to investigate the debris from the downed aircraft. The cart stopped and they began to interrogate the Frenchman.

185

By the sound of them, the German soldiers were both young and neither of them spoke much French. The farmer did nothing to disguise his hostility. Harry could imagine them pointing their rifles at the cart and wondered if they were going to start shooting or stick their bayonets in the hay. He'd certainly be doing that if he was them. He wondered whether to leap out with his hands in the air before they gored him. But he knew he couldn't do that. The man would be arrested for helping an American airman. They might shoot him, and Harry, on the spot. So Harry held his breath and tried not to sneeze. It had been building for a minute or two and this was the worst possible moment. He was itching terribly too, and aching to move a hand to scratch his leg.

The soldiers sounded bored. They couldn't be bothered to stick their bayonets in the hay, but they tried to talk more to the farmer. It sounded as though his defiance had riled them. One of them spoke aggressively and Harry heard what sounded like a scuffle.

The other soldier spoke in a conciliatory way.

Harry heard the horse deposit a heap of dung on to the road. The farmer laughed, as if to say, 'That's what he thinks of you.'

Harry heard muttering and curses, but the voices were walking away, and a moment later the cart began to clip-clop onward.

The rest of the journey was just noises: the muffled trundle of wooden wheels on mud and grass, then the rattle of cobblestones. He heard the farmer shout a greeting to someone and then the sound of gates being opened, then closed.

He felt his arm being shaken. '*Allez, allez.*'

In the brief moment between climbing out of the hay and being bustled inside again, Harry saw he was in the enclosed courtyard of another farm. He was bombarded with sensual delights. The warmth of the place was all enveloping, the smell of the wood-burning fire was delicious. And there were cooking smells too – baking bread and a meaty stew.

'This way,' said a female voice. A little Frenchwoman around the same age as the farmer quickly bundled him into a stairway down to the cellar. She introduced herself as Madame Laruelle. 'Now, monsieur, be quiet and wait here, please.'

Another voice cried out in delight. 'Harry Friedman! I thought you were dead.' It was Stearley. He ran up to Harry and gave him a great hug, even lifting him off the ground. 'I saw you falling. I lost you in the sky. I was hoping these guys would find you. They picked me up almost immediately.'

He slapped Harry's back again. 'Well some of us got out at least,' he said, suddenly sober.

Harry thought about the other non-coms – Skaggs, Hill, Dalinsky and Corrales were all dead. He was the only one of his buddies who had made it.

'Wonder where Bortz and LaFitte landed,' Stearley continued. 'Cain was badly wounded by flak – I think he was still in the Fortress when it went down. Jesus, what a day.'

'And Holberg?' asked Harry.

Stearley shook his head.

'He was determined to get *Macey May* back to England. That chewing out he got from Kittering about the ditching . . .' He stopped. 'Berg felt he ought to show the old bastard what he was made of by bringing a badly damaged Fortress back. Well, it cost him his life.'

The door at the top of the stairwell creaked open. A stern young man came down into the cellar and brusquely demanded to speak to each of them separately, telling Stearley to go upstairs and wait with the farmer and his wife.

Then he fired a series of questions at Harry, without even the hint of a smile.

'Who is the other *américain*?'

'Do you fly together?'

'What is 'is job?'

'Which plane do you fly?'

'Where is your airbase?'

Harry answered some of the questions, but told the man he was not allowed to tell him about the airbase. It was against regulations. After all, Harry didn't know who he was.

He thought this would make him angry, but he started to ask more personal questions instead.

'Tell me where you are from.'

'Where is the nearest public library to your 'ouse?'

'What are you parents' names?'

'How many brothers and sisters do you 'ave?'

Harry was all right with those. He knew the answers without thinking and answered them quickly. But then the young man said, 'Who's the coach for the New York Giants?'

Harry didn't know. He wasn't interested in football.

'Any true New Yorker would know the answer to that question.'

'I am a true New Yorker and I haven't got a clue,' he replied indignantly. 'We're not all interested in football. My sport's baseball. Ask me about the Brooklyn Dodgers, or the World Fair of 1939, and I'll tell you about that.'

That threw him. 'We 'ave to be careful. The Gestapo sometimes send us spies instead of real airmen. Now, you say you were in the bomber with this officer, so you 'ave known him several months?'

'We trained together in the States,' said Harry.

'Then I will just ask 'im a few more questions.'

Harry understood. He was well aware of the danger the Resistance were in.

The young man vanished, and Stearley returned five minutes later. 'Well, he was a charmer!' he joked. 'But I think they know we're the real thing.'

They heard the door to the cellar open again and this time it was the elderly French woman who crept downstairs. 'Are you angry?' she said to them. 'I am angry!'

Harry's heart sank for a moment. What on earth had they done? 'I'm sorry,' he said. 'Are we being too noisy?'

But she smiled. 'No, no. Are you angry? I bring you something to eat, yes?'

Harry and Stearley burst out laughing and she looked puzzled and a little hurt.

'Yes, yes, please, ma'am,' said Harry. '*Je suis très faim.*'

She corrected him with a kindly smile. '*J'ai très faim.*'

It was the finest meal Harry had eaten since he had arrived in Europe, maybe even in his life. Madame Laruelle even brought a carafe of red wine and three little mustard jars for glasses. Then she sat with them while they ate, occasionally shushing them when their conversation grew boisterous. Harry didn't like to drink much, but he loved that wine. Its rough edge complemented the rich stew to perfection.

Stearley proposed a toast 'To Life', and they clinked together their mustard jars.

At once Harry felt an overwhelming relief that he was still alive.

'Tonight you rest, and maybe tomorrow too,' said Madame Laruelle. She shrugged. 'Maybe a week. Then we try to get you back to England.'

Stearley turned serious. 'Please can you thank the gentleman who came to get me. It was a very dangerous thing to do.'

'Yes, monsieur,' she said, suddenly grave. 'My husband, he is a brave man. *Les Boches*, they shoot people who help the airmen. We saw your plane come down and we wondered if there were survivors. And lucky we got you before the *Boche* patrols. They don't kill the airmen. But they might have beaten you a little. Then off to prison camp.' She smiled 'We need you back in England and ready to fight.'

There was a creaking at the top of the stairs. '*Ahhh, Gérard,*' she said. '*Tu prends un verre de vin?*'

The farmer joined them with a shake of the hand and quickly knocked back a jar of the wine. He spoke to his wife, who turned to Harry and Stearley and said, 'Do you have photographs?'

They did. Harry and Stearley handed over their little passport-sized photos.

Madame and Monsieur Laruelle immediately began a hurried conversation.

'Is something wrong?' asked Stearley in French.

'*Je ne sais pas,*' said Madame Laruelle. 'These photographs – they are not quite right. The look is too bright, too smooth. We will leave them out in the weather and see if we can fade them. Then I visit a friend to get you some identity papers.'

'Are you worried about helping us?' asked Harry.

She gave him a warm smile. 'A little. But Gérard and I are old now. If they shoot us, they just end a long life a little sooner . . . But better for us if they don't.' She picked up her glass and clinked it with theirs. 'Still, to life, eh!'

CHAPTER 21

Northern France, October 17th, 1943

At the end of the third day, Madame Laruelle came down with two identity papers. They were well done, she explained, and it was important that the two of them learned the details so they could answer any question from a suspicious guard without hesitation. That night Harry and Stearley spent at least an hour memorising their new identities.

How old were they?

When were they born?

What was their occupation?

And most importantly, what was their name?

Stearley spoke much better French than Harry and coached him on his accent and how to pronounce those essential details as realistically as possible. Harry was beginning to like Stearley a lot more and felt guilty about how he and the other non-coms had judged him in the past.

On the next day they were shaken awake before first light. Harry immediately wondered if something was wrong and opened his eyes terrified he would see the green uniform of a German soldier. Then he noticed the sweet smell of baked bread and coffee. It was Madame Laruelle and she had brought them both a little breakfast.

'Today you leave here,' she said. 'Exciting, no? I will bring hot water to wash.'

They both nodded.

'We leave after one hour,' she said.

Then, almost as an afterthought, she added, 'Monsieur Laruelle has clothes for you. I bring *immédiatement.*'

Several of the clothes she bought were flecked in paint – perfect for their disguise as a couple of painters and decorators – Henri Leclerc and Louis Davout, according to their identity papers – on the way to Paris to do some work.

When they had washed and dressed in this assortment of cast-offs, the two airmen crept up the cellar stairs and knocked gingerly on the door. It opened to reveal an extraordinary sight.

Madame Laruelle was wearing an outlandish outfit that almost made Harry laugh out loud, but he realised at once this was a disguise. She had a flouncy peasant dress and a great straw hat with several feathers in it. She also carried a large shoulder bag with a half-drunk bottle of wine poking out of one corner.

'*C'est pour la Milice ou les allemands,*' her husband said.

'Milice?' said Harry to Stearley.

'French guys – they're Nazi sympathisers. Set up to fight the Resistance.'

Harry noticed the rank odour of sweat and unwashed clothes. Most of all, Madame Laruelle smelt of stale wine.

'You have to show your passes, yes?' she announced. 'Well, when we reach a German checkpoint I'm going to distract the soldiers, so they let you both through without inspection.'

Harry wondered if this dressing-up would be enough to fox the Germans or collaborators, but there was something about Madame Laruelle that made him trust her. Whatever she was up to, she had done it before and it had worked.

'So where are we going?' Stearley asked.

'Hesdin. It's a little town a few kilometres from here.'

'You know, we have no real idea where we are,' said Stearley.

'You're about thirty kilometres due east from the coast. Seventy kilometres north is Calais. Now, here is your route. You need a connection to Amiens. There's a contact at the railway station. You will call him Jacques. He'll take you to Paris. Then someone else will take over. You're going back to England through the Pyrenees, *mes enfants*. It's the surest route.'

'But that means travelling the length of France,' said Stearley, his voice betraying his unease. 'Isn't it easier to get to the coast here, then across the Channel?'

'You must trust us, Lieutenant,' she said firmly. 'Believe me, getting you through to Spain where you can contact the British Consulate there, is the safest, surest route. It's in Bilbao, near the border. There are other ways, of course, but this is the one we use.'

194

Harry felt deflated. He too had imagined they would be taken to the coast and picked up by a boat or submarine. Some sort of journey that would see them back in England in a few days. What Madame Laruelle was proposing sounded like an ordeal, a journey that might take weeks or months, where their lives would be in danger every minute of the day and night. But who was he to argue? He had to trust these brave people completely.

Madame Laruelle passed them each a small bag with a change of clothing, and a few francs for emergencies. '*Alors, maintenant, allons-y*,' she announced.

They left the safety of the farmhouse just as the sun was peeping over the horizon, and the first thing Madame Laruelle did was reach down into the mud and smear her face. Whatever was going to happen next was anyone's guess.

The light grew in the sky, revealing a few dark clouds but not enough to threaten a deluge. Madame Laruelle said they should now walk separately. They would be in the small town of Hesdin in the next half-hour and it would not do to be seen walking with her. She told them when they reached the town they should stay thirty seconds behind her and make sure they were next in line when they reached the checkpoint.

So Harry and Stearley held back as she put a brisk distance between herself and them.

It was light when they crossed the brow of a hill and saw the spires and rooftops of Hesdin before them. In the main route into the town there was a checkpoint – with a striped pole barrier across the road, and a sentry box. Several German soldiers were there, checking the passes of the trickle of arrivals wanting to get into the town that early morning.

Madame Laruelle turned her back and carefully splashed a little wine down her blouse. They closed up the distance separating them, hoping no one else would reach the checkpoint and get between them and her.

The plan worked. There they were, right behind her, with a couple of young women in front showing their passes.

Madame Laruelle watched the soldiers' gaze follow the girls as they walked into town. When they turned to her, she stumbled unsteadily on her feet and got out her wine, pulling out the half-inserted cork with her teeth. She offered it to them both, suppressed a burp and took a swig when they recoiled.

Then she put a hand on the tallest one's belt and drew him towards her, looking as though she was about to plant a large kiss on his cheek. The soldier pushed her away, roughly enough for her to fall to the ground. The bottle of wine smashed and she began to wail. Both soldiers started to curse at her in German. Clearly neither of them spoke much French. That was good, thought Harry. They would not be inclined to engage him or Stearley in conversation.

One soldier beckoned Stearley and Harry forward. At that moment, Madame Laruelle began to wail again, something about being an old woman, and tugged at the soldiers' uniforms. She seemed utterly distraught and Harry marvelled at how she was carrying off this act.

She held out a hand imploringly. One of the sentries relented. He hauled her to her feet and shoved her in the direction of the town centre.

The other one took the briefest look at the airmen's passes and hurriedly waved them through. Behind them, a busload of workers was approaching. The soldiers wanted to be ready for them.

They kept their distance and neither spoke. But they did catch each other's eyes when Stearley suppressed a snigger, and they instantly realised they were on the verge of hysterical laughter. Harry could imagine telling this anecdote to his friends and even grandchildren for the rest of his life.

Madame Laruelle was careful to ensure they kept her in sight as they made their way through the cobbled streets of Hesdin and through the main square. Over on the other side was a railway station. Madame Laruelle immediately went over to the fountain and splashed her face in the stream of water that emerged from a heavy iron pipe.

Harry and Stearley looked at each other, as if to say, 'What happens now?'

A voice behind startled them. '*Bonjour, messieurs, vous êtes les peintres en bâtiment?*'

They turned round to see a man of around thirty dressed in workman's clothes.

'*Venez, le train va partir dans dix minutes.*' Harry understood that – they had ten minutes to catch the train.

Harry looked over to Madame Laruelle but she had already gone. Then he saw her making her way out the other end of the square. Obviously there were to be no goodbyes. It made perfect sense, of course. Nothing to arouse suspicion. But he was sad that he was not able to thank her and her husband for their enormous courage and generosity.

The man ordered train tickets for the three of them, behaving as though he was the foreman and they were the apprentices. '*Venez.*' He beckoned them to follow him. They hurried over the bridge to Platform 2. Already, from above the railway line, Harry could see an approaching plume of smoke.

CHAPTER 22

October 18th, 1943

The first part of the journey away from Hesdin was simple enough and the carriage they travelled in was empty.

'The change at Amiens is easy – one platform to another, but there will be checks on the train. I will speak to the guard or the soldiers . . . you pretend to be asleep.'

Then he told them in great detail what their Paris courier would look like and what she would say to them and what they should reply. This would establish for both parties that they really were who they were supposed to be.

'Then, no conversation,' said Jacques. 'It is the quickest way to the firing squad, believe me.'

He paused to let his words sink in, then continued. 'The Gestapo, and our own Milice – they are very cunning. You can trust no one. Even the French police or railway men. No one wears a badge saying they are a *collaborateur*.'

As the train rattled along, Harry stared out at the autumn countryside. It still had its own melancholy beauty. He thought about Tilly working at her factory back in England. She must have found out the *Macey May* had not returned from Schweinfurt when she came to the Saturday dance.

He hoped she had been upset and concerned about him, but he wondered if she had just shrugged and spent the rest of the evening in the arms of another airman. When he wasn't daydreaming, he pretended to doze. The carriage was filling up and this was the best way to avoid any awkward conversation.

Much to Harry's relief, the journey to Amiens passed without incident. The ticket inspector didn't speak to them when he checked their tickets, and the train arrived in Paris on time. At Gare du Nord Jacques walked on ahead and they waited a minute before they followed. This was not a journey where you said goodbye. It went against Harry's every instinct. These people were risking their lives. He wanted to show his gratitude.

They made their way down the platform, discreetly scanning the concourse for German soldiers. There were a couple close to the main exit, along with two French inspectors.

The station was busy and full of impatient travellers keen to be on their way. No one was paying a great deal of attention to two young men who looked as if they had come to Paris to do a decorating job.

The queue at the end of the platform was dense and impatient. When Harry got to the inspector he handed over his ticket. The man paused. Something was wrong. He could see it in his face. He looked Harry straight in the eye, then he smiled and handed the ticket back. '*Bonne chance, monsieur*,' he said under his breath.

Harry was right behind Stearley and had to bite his lip so as not to blurt out, 'What the hell was that about?'

They were to leave the station by its main exit and look for a fountain to the right of the square in front of them. Their instructions had been very explicit.

A French girl, maybe still in her teens, stood at the fountain.

'That can't be her,' whispered Stearley. 'She's far too young.'

But she exactly matched the description of the girl Natalie who they were supposed to meet. She was carrying a green leather handbag and wore a crocodile brooch studded with green crystals on the left lapel of her cream coat.

Her pale complexion stood in sharp contrast to the dark curve of her eyebrows and the wisps of black hair than curled around her face. Harry thought she was very beautiful. She had her hair tied back in a ponytail, a style many girls would find unflattering, but with her it just accentuated her cheekbones, huge hazel eyes in her oval face, and strong, sharp nose.

Stearley whispered, 'What a doll!' Harry flinched. What did Stearley think he was doing speaking to him in English out in the street?

She smiled at them both. Before they could speak she said in French the exact words Jacques had told them she would say: 'It is still warm in Toulouse. I should have stayed there.'

Stearley trotted out their pre-arranged reply in passable French. 'Yes, but it will be warm here tomorrow, I think.'

He had practised that over and over. Harry had watched him mouthing the words on the train. He got the feeling that Natalie was someone Stearley really wanted to impress, and that made him feel uneasy.

They took the Métro to Raspail, Natalie standing a distance away from them, but still close enough for them to see when she got off. Harry noticed a few people staring at them, and wondered if they looked different or suspicious.

It was a short journey. After a brisk walk through wide boulevards of imposing apartment blocks they arrived at an elaborate entrance where she swiftly ushered them into a marble lobby. She nodded briefly to the concierge and they took the lift all the way to the sixth floor.

As the lift creaked its way up the floors Harry could tell Stearley was bursting to speak to her. Harry had heard about 'femmes fatales' and seen them in the movies. There was something unreal about Natalie and he caught himself wondering if they'd be better off with someone not quite so eye-catching.

The apartment overlooked the street. The rooms were generous in size, with high ceilings, although they were sparsely furnished.

'Here we are, gentlemen,' she said in perfect English, with a pronounced French accent. 'Now, as you are supposed to be decorators, I suggest you do some painting.

Make a bit of noise. You can have a go at that wall over there.' She pointed to the broadest wall in the living room. 'We mustn't give the neighbours any grounds for suspicion.'

Harry wondered if she was joking, but it appeared not. 'So, we should use real paint!' said Stearley, trying to mask his disbelief.

'Yes, monsieur, but just a bit. It's rationed of course, like everything else. Just enough to give the room and yourself the smell of paint. Don't worry, you won't be here long.'

Stearley was anxious to change the subject. 'So, where did you learn to speak English so well?' He gave her his best Clark Gable smile.

She wagged a finger. 'Ahhh, Monsieur. Please, we must not talk about anything that isn't strictly necessary. I'm sure you understand.' For the first time she smiled. He held her gaze longer than was strictly proper.

Natalie glanced at her watch. 'Now I must be going. I will be back tomorrow with some food for you. Meanwhile, I have to get you more travel passes. You must be patient, gentlemen. We will try to get you on your way as soon as possible.'

She turned to go, pausing by the door. 'There is food in the kitchen. *Bon appétit!*' Then she was gone.

There was nothing to do, other than pretend to be painting but they soon ran out of paint. The lieutenant tried to read some French books, but without a dictionary to check those words he didn't understand, he soon lost interest. Harry had nothing to do at all. Natalie had warned them against standing looking out of the window. Anything that would cause suspicion would mean imprisonment for them and death to their helpers.

CHAPTER 23

Paris, October 19th, 1943

The following day Natalie returned with a package from the chemist.

'Harry, I think we should change your hair colour – make it lighter, yes?' she said.

He was aghast. 'What for?'

'You have very dark hair, and it's curly. The Germans may think you look Jewish,' she said matter-of-factly.

Harry nodded. She sounded so determined he didn't dare argue.

'The Germans, and our own Milice, have been arresting and deporting Jews for over a year. We know they send them east, and no one ever comes back, or is heard from again, so we fear the worst. They may treat you different as an *américain*, but they still might think you are a Jew to be arrested if they see you in the street.'

Harry was taking all this in with a mounting sense of horror. They had all heard stories about the Nazi persecution of the Jews in occupied Europe. Here he was now facing the same dangers himself.

'So, let us cut your hair and then we will use a little hair lightener,' she said.

She cut his hair in the living room, with a sheet spread on the floor, and made a pretty good job of it. 'I used to do my brother and sister,' she said. Then she shook her head to indicate he was not to ask her about them.

The hair-dyeing business was not as complicated as he thought it might be. She rubbed a chemical paste into his scalp and eyebrows, then held his head over the bathroom sink to rinse it away. 'The trick is not to leave it in too long.'

Harry was enjoying having her near to him as she cut and dyed his hair. He could see Stearley was watching the whole process closely. He offered to help but she briskly refused.

The dye did the trick. His hair was several shades lighter – still dark, but not the deep black it was naturally.

After that the days took on a dreary monotony. They turned into a week and Harry found it difficult to remember which day it actually was. Natalie visited every other day, with bread and dried meat, and some apples and sometimes potatoes. She apologised about the lack of variety in their food, but otherwise would not be drawn into conversation.

When she was not there Stearley started to talk about Natalie all the time. Mostly she wore the same cream coat every day, but occasionally she would turn up in a black coat. Sometimes she wore a red beret, sometimes a black one. It was a subject that interested Stearley inordinately.

Harry was alarmed by the lieutenant's growing obsession with her. Every time she visited, his eyes would never leave her. And after she left he always made the same joke about having to take a cold shower.

Harry wondered if he ought to say something to him about this. But it was all too embarrassing. Besides, he didn't want to fall out with his lieutenant.

One late afternoon, when it had been raining non-stop, there was a rattle at the door. Natalie came in looking bedraggled. But she announced she had managed to find them some lamb cutlets and intended to cook them a fine dinner.

'I even have a nice bottle of wine,' she said. 'And a little butter for our potatoes.'

The food they had that evening was delicious, and Harry found himself thinking of John Hill and how much he would have enjoyed it. Natalie fried the chops in garlic and herbs and prepared green beans and buttered potatoes. Harry could picture John there in the kitchen, leaning over her shoulder watching how she cooked. He couldn't believe he wasn't there in the world any more.

As they ate, Natalie had to keep telling them to be a little quieter. Stearley, especially, was getting boisterous as the bottle slowly emptied and she was obviously worried about the neighbours overhearing their conversation. Harry had barely drunk at all back home in Brooklyn, but the wine went very well with it all, and he was getting a taste for it.

After they had eaten she said, 'I have some news. Some good. Some not so. First the not so good. You will have to stay here for at least another week. Your passes are not in order and we need to do them again.'

Their faces fell. So this was what this was about. A treat to keep them in good spirits.

But then she smiled and fished out two books from her bag. 'The good news ... I have a present for you both.'

She placed the books on the table. John Steinbeck's *The Grapes of Wrath* and Margaret Mitchell's *Gone with the Wind*.

She searched their faces. 'I hope you have not read them already.' She pushed the Mitchell towards Stearley.

'I thought you would enjoy this one, monsieur,' she said with a smile.

Harry laughed at her joke about Stearley's likeness to Clark Gable, who had starred in the film of *Gone with the Wind* – a global cinema sensation in the year the war broke out.

'And also, I have a pack of cards. That will help, yes? Now I have to go. I leave you the washing-up, if you don't mind!'

The two airmen did the dishes together, both of them full of wine-fuelled bonhomie and good cheer.

'What a girl,' said Stearley. 'Isn't she something!'

'Have you read those books?' asked Harry. He'd read *Gone with the Wind* – hadn't everybody? – but he hadn't read the Steinbeck. He didn't care though. He was desperate for something to keep him occupied.

'I never read the "Wind" book,' said Stearley. 'Seen the film though.'

Harry was reluctant to feed the lieutenant's vanity but he couldn't help himself. 'I liked her Clark Gable joke,' he said.

Stearley gave a little smile. 'I'm winning her round, Harry. Just you see!'

Natalie arrived with more books a few days later, but that didn't stop them climbing the walls with boredom. Both of them were finding it difficult to sleep and Harry was often troubled by nightmares where he was trapped in a burning plane. He kept flashing back to his final moments with his friend John. He wished he could have saved that photograph of his girl Shirley. Then when all this was over, he could have sent it back to her and told her it was the last thing he saw. His thoughts often drifted to the other guys in the *Macey May* who had been killed. It was almost too much to take in – these boys who had been flesh and blood a few days before were now just a memory.

The weather took a turn for the better. For three days there was bright autumn sunshine, and the days were warm enough to have a window open. It was like being in prison, not being able to go out.

Now when Natalie visited, Stearley and Harry pleaded to be let outside. Eventually she gave in and said she would take them out for a short walk on Saturday evening. There were usually lots of people out on the street and many of them would be drunk. The Milice and the Germans would have enough everyday ill behaviour to watch out for already.

After she'd gone, Stearley was in unusually good spirits. They could find a café, he confided to Harry, and he would ask her to dance. That would sweep her off her feet.

'But won't we look ridiculous?' said Harry. 'A couple of decorators out with a beautiful girl.'

'Hey, Harry, you've got style or you haven't!' he replied. 'We'll look fine.'

True to her word, she turned up on Saturday evening. Harry was amused to see she had made herself look as dowdy as possible and wore an old grey coat clearly in need of a brush-down. Whether this was to blend in with the two scruffy decorators she was accompanying, or send a clear message to Stearley that she wasn't interested in him, Harry didn't know.

But it was marvellous being out, even on a frosty autumnal evening. The air had a crisp sparkle that made them feel very much alive. They walked along a busy street and then the length of a park that had closed for the evening. Harry was very taken by the elegance of Paris, with its wide cobbled streets and great tall apartment blocks, built a hundred years or so before. He was fascinated by this city and desperately wanted to know more about it, but Natalie had forbidden them to speak out in the street.

After they had strolled around the twilight streets for half an hour they came across a café bar where dance music could be heard. Stearley broke her no-talking rule and whispered, 'So, Natalie, will you come and dance?'

She was frosty. '*Monsieur, vous êtes fou – c'est impossible.*' Harry understood that – 'You must be mad.'

There was an ugly silence. '*Venez, rentrons a l'appartement,*' she said abruptly.

Stearley hadn't expected her to turn him down; Harry could see it in his face. As they walked back they passed several other cafés where the music from a small jazz band or a gramophone drifted out into the street. They reached a crossroads close to their safe house.

Now Stearley was fuming and Harry hoped he wasn't going to do anything stupid.

As they neared the apartment, Stearley announced, 'I'm sick of being cooped up in that dreary place. I need to stretch my legs some more. I'll be back later.'

With that he walked off down a side street. Natalie and Harry watched him go with mounting unease. Then a coldness came over her. She looked around to make sure they would not be overheard.

'So . . . he's on his own,' she whispered quietly. 'You and me, we will go to another safe house. When he gets back, there will be no one there.'

Harry thought about going after him, but before he could do anything else, they saw Stearley turn round to look back at them as if he had been expecting them to come after him. Not looking where he was going, he bumped straight into a German soldier. There under the lamplight Natalie and Harry watched as the two exchanged words, then the German pointed his rifle straight at Stearley.

CHAPTER 24

What happened next astonished them. Stearley punched the German soldier so hard he collapsed on the ground, out cold. Worse was to come. The lieutenant turned on his heels and ran back towards the two of them.

Natalie told Harry to walk away as fast as he could without being conspicuous. Stearley caught up soon enough.

They walked the next few streets in angry silence. She led them back to the apartment, and when she had bolted the door she gave Stearley a look of cold hatred.

'You idiot,' she spat at him as quietly as her rage would allow. 'Why did you punch him?'

He seemed rather pleased with himself. 'Kraut walking into me threw me. I said, "Watch out, pal." Then I realised I'd spoken to him in English. He raised his rifle so I knocked him out. Hope I broke his jaw.'

'Well,' said Natalie icily, 'I'm going to leave you and I'm not coming back. You can fend for yourself. I suspect you won't have to for long though, because the Germans will be here searching every house in the next hour. And you

213

can spend the rest of the war in a prison camp. Well done, Lieutenant Stearley. You're a credit to your nation.'

He stared open-mouthed at her rage.

'Was that why you wanted to go for a walk? So you could ask me to dance? Do you not understand how treacherous this business is? Do you not realise that if you are noticed then I will be arrested and almost certainly tortured and shot?'

Shaking her head in disgust, she left without another word.

Harry expected an apology from Stearley, but the lieutenant was still looking immensely pleased with himself. 'She'll be back,' he said.

Harry didn't know what to say. He wanted to hit Stearley, but he knew hitting an officer was a very serious offence. What could he do to make him realise he was behaving like an idiot? He took himself away to another room and seethed in silence.

Expecting the streets to be full of German soldiers with dogs and torches, and thinking every creak and bang in the night was someone knocking on the door, Harry was too tense to sleep. Stearley went out like a light, entirely indifferent to the trouble he had brought upon them.

But when Harry did fall asleep and then woke around three in the morning he realised there had been no house-to-house searches after all. The Germans had not reacted as Natalie had predicted. Perhaps Stearley had got away with it.

There was enough food in the apartment for breakfast the next morning, which was good as Harry was not looking forward to having to argue with Stearley about whether they should go out and buy their breakfast in a café with the few francs they had between them. He had grown to like Stearley in these long days holed up here. But now he was really beginning to detest him.

'What are we going to do?' he asked Stearley after they had finished off the last of a stale baguette.

'Wait. She'll be back. They won't leave us here –'

There was a knock at the door.

Harry tiptoed to look through the peephole. There was a Frenchman standing there, a few feet back so anyone looking at him could see him clearly. Harry and Stearley both agreed it was not the way they'd expect the Gestapo or the Milice to behave. Stearley opened the door.

The man walked right in. 'Lieutenant Stearley?' he asked in impeccable English, once the door was shut.

Stearley nodded, and before he could say a word, the man punched him hard in the stomach. Stearley collapsed on the floor gasping for air, writhing in agony.

'If this happens again, expect the worst,' said the man. 'And I'll tell you this, I'd happily shoot you myself.'

Stearley remained on the floor.

'You are not to leave the apartment. If you do, then you are on your own,' the man said. He turned and left without another word.

Stearley lay on the floor for a full five minutes before he found the strength to haul himself up. 'She'll be back,' he said to Harry. 'I'll bet you a croissant she'll be back!'

Harry bit his tongue as he felt the anger building up inside him. He wanted to tell Stearley the man was right. He was being more than foolish. But Harry knew they shouldn't fall out. Besides, Stearley was his commanding officer now Holberg was dead. That still counted for something, surely.

A while later, when his anger had abated, Harry did manage to raise the subject indirectly. 'You know, if we're arrested, and the Nazis discover I'm a Jew, it's going to be far worse for me than it is for you.'

Stearley thought about it for a brief moment, then said, 'Don't worry about it. You're an American and you're protected by the Geneva Convention.'

It was clear to Harry that Stearley hadn't connected his own behaviour with what Harry had said about being a Jew at all. He fumed silently, cursing the lieutenant's arrogance.

Later that afternoon they had another visitor – a large French lady in late middle age carrying a grey shopping bag. She let herself in and they were both startled to see this stranger in their midst. She barely spoke to them, just dropped off provisions and then left.

Three days later they were dozing in the afternoon, wondering what to do next, when they heard the front door open. Natalie was standing there, eyes blazing with anger, clutching a bag of provisions. 'My superior officer tells me I have to carry on with you as we have lost another operative. But I will not tolerate any foolishness. Do I make myself understood?'

Stearley stood up and walked over to her. For one awful moment Harry thought he was going to try to embrace her, but he didn't. He stood a respectful distance away and said, 'Mademoiselle, I apologise unreservedly.'

She nodded, and Harry thought he saw the ghost of a smile flicker across her face. He liked Natalie, although she frightened him too. She was beautiful, she was resourceful and clever, but she had this ruthless streak in her eye that he had never seen in any other girl.

'Tonight we are going to take a train down to Châteauroux,' she said. 'Austerlitz is our station. We'll walk. It's not far. And it's always good not to have to go through unnecessary checkpoints on the Métro. So we need to leave here at six to catch the seven o'clock train. Help yourself to provisions – I have bread and cheese and ham, and eat as much as you can because I'm not sure when we'll be getting some more.'

When she had left, Stearley had a smug smile on his lips. 'I'll bet you a week's pay, yours against mine, she'll come round before we get to the Pyrenees. All these opportunities . . .'

Harry saw red. Despite the fact that Stearley was maybe eight inches taller, he threw himself at him. 'Are you totally crazy?' he shouted, his anger getting the better of him.

Taken by surprise, the lieutenant was knocked to the floor. Harry grabbed him by the lapels. 'They'll kill you, didn't you hear that? And if your stupid behaviour gets us all arrested, then Natalie will be executed . . .'

Harry let go, expecting Stearley to say something conciliatory. But this unexpected attack had riled him. In an instant he swung a fist up and hit Harry on the side of the face, sending him sprawling across the floor.

They both lay there for a few moments. Harry noticed the side of his face was beginning to ache and winced when he touched it. Already it had started to swell.

Stearley stood and offered him a hand. 'I'm sorry, Harry,' he said. 'All this being cooped up is getting to us. Come on, let me bathe that.'

Harry sat on the side of the bath while Stearley squeezed out a dishcloth and gave it to him to press against his bruise. Then he left him on his own.

When Harry looked in the mirror he could see a purple bruise just beneath his left eye. It no longer throbbed as much as it had done, but it made him look like a hood who had been in a fight. When the apartment door opened they expected to see Natalie all ready to take them. It was her, but she was wide-eyed with fear. 'Look out of the window,' she said. 'The Gestapo are out on the street, I'm sure of it.' The doorbell buzzed before she said another word.

She ignored it. There was a persistent series of buzzes.

She peered cautiously out of the window. Three

men wearing leather coats were gathered around the apartment entrance. A squad of Wehrmacht soldiers stood behind them.

They heard other buzzers in the apartments around them. Someone was going to let them in at any moment.

'Quickly,' said Natalie, and they followed her out and headed up to the roof.

There was a skylight at the very top and a little wooden ladder leading up to it. She vaulted up and immediately began to force it open. Before she squeezed out she said, 'We must stay on the rear side of the roof. Otherwise they'll see us from below.'

She beckoned impatiently for the airmen to follow. Stearley gestured for Harry to go next. Below came the sound of rapid footsteps on the stairs. As Harry squeezed out he heard the crash of splintering wood. They would be into that apartment in seconds. Stearley followed as soon as Harry had gone through. He had the presence of mind to shut the skylight behind him.

The roof was a dizzying height above the streets and the skylight had brought them out on to curving tiles that sloped down to a shallow parapet. 'Go slowly,' said Natalie. They gingerly picked their way down the steep curve of the roof. Harry lost his grip on the tiles, which were still damp from the afternoon rain, and slipped down, lurching alarmingly as his feet made contact with the parapet. Stearley, right behind him, grabbed his sleeve, pulling him back from the edge.

'We have to jump to the next building,' said Natalie. 'Just do it. We have only a few seconds to get away.'

They edged over, keeping their backs to the wall, trying not to look down at the back street far below. Natalie went first, throwing her bag across, then leaping over the gap with barely a second thought.

Harry flinched at the size of the gap. It must be at least four feet. 'Hurry,' she snapped. He took a short run-up and launched himself across; his foot just about reached the parapet on the far roof. She grabbed his hand and they both fell over against the sharp sloping slates. Harry heard a tile crack and thought maybe wood in the eaves had split. Stearley followed and made the jump easily enough.

There was no skylight. Instead there were roof windows. Natalie wasted no time edging up to one and peering through. She opened her bag and took out a revolver, carefully smashing a small pane of glass and flipping open the handle.

The noise drew the attention of the residents of the rooftop apartment, and when Harry and Stearley reached the window they could see Natalie standing there, pointing her gun at two elderly occupants. Harry thought they were sisters by the look of them.

She spoke to them rapidly in French. Harry could not understand, although he did pick up the word 'Gestapo'.

They looked at her, frozen with fear. She spoke again, waving her hand impatiently.

The elder of the two sisters began to babble and held out a key.

Natalie snatched it from her and they took the stairs two at a time, not even thinking to be quiet.

There was a door to the back alley and it opened as soon as Natalie turned the key. Peering cautiously up the street she beckoned them out and told them to walk fast. 'If the Gestapo notice a running figure, they will know at once who to chase,' she said with impeccable logic.

But one of the Gestapo was already out on the roof and a shot rang out, shattering a cobblestone right by Harry's foot.

They ran out through the back alley and into a maze of small streets. Natalie obviously knew the area well, for she seemed to be running with a clear purpose. After a couple of minutes she knocked on the door of a house on a side street. After a few moments a young woman answered.

Natalie spoke rapidly in French; it sounded to Harry as though she was pleading to be let in. He recognised the word 'Gestapo' again.

The door slammed in their faces.

CHAPTER 25

They hurried on until they reached a park. The keeper's bell was ringing, letting everyone know it was time to leave for the evening.

'Perfect,' said Natalie, surveying the empty gardens. There was a large evergreen close to the entrance and, when they were sure no one was watching them, they dived in there.

'Now don't even breathe,' she said. 'We must be very patient.'

They crouched still and silent in the prickly lower branches of the tree. After a couple of minutes they heard running footsteps and the barking of angry dogs. Peering through the foliage, Harry could see several German soldiers running past the gates, accompanied by men in leather overcoats. He hoped those dogs hadn't picked up a scent. That would be it for all of them.

But the running men didn't stop and the sound of barking dogs vanished into the distance.

Then the park keeper locked up for the night and left.

'Why did they raid the apartment?' whispered Harry. 'How did they know?'

'Maybe one of the neighbours got suspicious,' she said. 'We should not have kept you there so long. Especially after the lieutenant's attack on the soldier.'

In an instant he thought of the fight he and Stearley had had. He had done the shouting, although their scuffling must have been noticed by the downstairs neighbours at least.

'But why would the French betray us to the Nazis?' asked Harry.

Natalie looked at him impatiently. 'Come, monsieur, there are fascists everywhere. In France before the war we had our own Action Française party. Just like the British had their Blackshirts and you Americans had your German American Bund. There are always people who will support fascism. I'm pleased to tell you most of us despise the Milice and the Vichy collaborators. They will pay when this is all over.'

Then she said, 'You've bruised your face. Did that happen just now?'

'No,' said Harry, then immediately felt like he was telling tales. He shook his head and said no more. She could draw her own conclusions.

'What do we do now?' asked Stearley. Harry sensed he was anxious to change the conversation.

She eyed him coolly. 'We cannot take the train. We will go to another safe house. We will go when I think it's safe.'

She looked at her watch. 'We can't wait too long here. Certainly we need to be away before the eleven o'clock curfew.'

Hours passed and it was only after the local clock struck ten that the street was empty enough for them to emerge from their hiding place. As they clambered over the park railings Stearley picked up Natalie by the waist to help her up, as if she weighed no more than a bag of shopping. Natalie accepted this help matter-of-factly.

Their new safe house was a ten-minute walk away in another apartment in a side road off one of the grand boulevards. As before, they walked apart but keeping one another in sight, so that no one would think they were together. Harry was completely lost and couldn't imagine what he would do if he became separated from Natalie.

The two airmen watched her enter and then followed through the door she had left ajar. They hurried up three flights of stairs and the elderly couple who opened the door looked immediately fearful.

'*Vite, vite,*' said Natalie, picking up on their unease.

Harry and Stearley were shown into the living room and stood there awkwardly as they overheard uneasy conversation in the kitchen. The couple were tight-lipped, not remotely like Madame and Monsieur Laruelle. They were obviously very unhappy about having the two Americans in their apartment.

Natalie came into the room. She spoke to them quickly under her breath. 'You will stay here one night only. Now,

224

we need new tickets and permits.' Then, without a further word, she left them.

Natalie returned at 2 p.m. the next day, not before Harry and Stearley had spent an uncomfortable morning. No more was said about their fight, and Harry even thanked the lieutenant for saving him on the roof. But there was an unease between them now, a trust that had been broken.

The couple they were staying with made it clear they had no food for them, but they did bring a change of clothes – rough workmen's apparel. At least it was freshly laundered. The old lady beckoned for them to throw their old clothes in her laundry basket.

'Today we make a short journey – to Le Mans from Gare Montparnasse,' said Natalie. 'On the train we must sit apart of course. When it is time to get off, I will stand up and check my hair in the mirror in the carriage, yes? You get off at the next stop, even if I don't get off. It's very important that you remember this.

'And don't for a second make any gesture or contact that would let someone know we are all travelling together. Sit opposite each other, not together. When one of you goes to sleep, then the other should stay awake. If you start talking in your sleep, you will give yourself away. So wake them, yes?'

Harry wilted when he heard this. He was so tired he could have slept on a marble floor or in a puddle of water. Stearley looked exhausted too. He bet he'd pull rank if they discussed who would fall asleep first. Harry resolved to be sly and not even mention it. As soon as they sat down, then that would be it. Over and out.

She fished into her bag and brought out two newspapers. 'You can have one each. Read them throughout the journey. It'll discourage any conversation from your fellow passengers.' One paper was German, the other Dutch. It was a good move, unless someone Dutch or German was sitting next to you.

Stearley took the German paper, which was brave. With so many German soldiers around, the chances of a German starting a conversation with you were far higher.

As they prepared to leave, the atmosphere in the apartment lightened considerably. The old lady wished them '*Bonne chance*' and pressed a paper bag into Natalie's hands. Even the old man gave them a hearty handshake. Their relief was palpable.

Out in the street they walked alone, in sight of each other. Harry hoped it was not too far to the station and tried his best not to look anxious and lost. Stearley was walking behind Natalie and Harry was appalled at one point to hear him wolf whistle at a small group of French girls, sitting in their fur coats, enjoying a coffee and cigarette outside a café.

As they waited for their train in the towering station concourse, a sprightly young man in a smart suit came up to Harry and began to chat away. Harry froze. The language was not one he recognised. It was certainly not French or

German. Then he realised the man was probably Dutch, and had assumed Harry was too, because of the newspaper he carried. As he talked, Harry wondered whether to whisper, 'I'm American, go away!' But in an instant he calculated that anyone this healthy and smart was almost certainly a Dutch collaborator, here in Paris to do business with the Nazis and their French supporters.

Harry shook his head and waved the man away. A couple of German soldiers walked by, clearly taking an interest in what looked like the start of an argument, or even a fight. Harry felt himself go hot and cold with fear.

Natalie rushed up to him. 'Hendrick! Hendrick van Houten!!! *Mon cher ami!!! Venez, vous avez le temps pour un café avant le départ de votre train?*'

With that she whisked him away to one of the cafés on the side of the concourse. She bought him a coffee and ten minutes later they were in the queue with Stearley, two or three people apart, waiting to board the train alongside hundreds of impatient passengers. Harry had begun to realise that big queues and impatient people were the fugitive's friend. The platform inspectors, and the German sentries who watched over them, waved them through with only the slightest glance at their passes.

If they were lucky, they would get to Le Mans by mid-evening. If not, it could be early the next morning. Either way, it was going to be a long night.

CHAPTER 26

Le Mans, November 8th, 1943

Jean-Pierre, Natalie's controller in the Resistance, had come down to Le Mans that very morning, shortly after meeting with her. There was work to do with the local Resistance – contacts to make after the last Nazi round-up of the Resistance cell there. Four of his friends here had recently been executed. And Jean-Pierre had messages to transmit to the Special Operation Executive back in England – the branch of the British Secret Service that worked closely with Resistance groups in occupied Europe. It was safer in Le Mans, he always felt. There were too many Nazi signal-tracking vans in Paris. He'd heard of friends there getting that ominous knocking at the door five minutes into a transmission. Things were slacker here.

He had met the two Americans at that apartment in Paris, now compromised and unusable, but at least he had taught Stearley a lesson. He hoped it would make him behave more responsibly. He didn't trust him though. He'd had similar trouble with a British officer a few months back. Nearly got two of his men caught when he started to chat up a woman in a café right by the Arc de Triomphe.

Jean-Pierre was quite prepared to die ferrying these flyers back to England, but not for someone else's foolishness.

He tapped out the day's news for London. The two flyers were safe and he was expecting them in Le Mans shortly, but it had been a close thing. One of them, the co-pilot, was causing no end of trouble. He was flirting with the courier and taking terrible risks to impress her. And he'd had a fight with another escaper. Immediate advice was required.

The message came back from SOE almost instantly. Jean-Pierre flinched at its stark brutality.

They were lucky with the train from Montparnasse. There were no long delays, and they pulled into the station at Le Mans around ten o'clock that evening.

The place felt quite different from Paris. More relaxed. There were a few German guards at the station, but they seemed bored and took little time checking the passengers' passes.

Harry and Stearley followed Natalie down the dark streets. She walked for maybe twenty minutes into the centre, and they found themselves in a district of old timbered houses.

Natalie unlocked a creaking door in a drab plaster-fronted terrace. When they caught up, she was waiting for them in the darkened hall.

She beckoned them to follow her upstairs, where there was a small apartment on the top floor.

'Two rooms – you can have one each. Wait here until I come to collect you.'

Then she left without another word.

Natalie returned in the dead of night. It had been a difficult journey, in which they had narrowly avoided a roadblock. She felt uneasy. On edge. Outside on the landing she could hear Stearley snoring but he stopped when the door to his room creaked open. She crept in, holding a single candle. He was in a deep sleep, a little smile playing around his lips, and she had to nudge him several times to fully wake him. When he opened his eyes, he looked surprised, delighted and then crestfallen in the space of an instant.

'What's happening?' he asked.

She put her finger to her lips. 'Come with me,' she whispered.

'Where are we going?' he asked.

'I will tell you on the way,' she said. 'I'll wait outside the door while you get dressed.'

She stood on the landing, noting that the younger one in the other room was sleeping soundly. She could hear his gentle snoring. She wondered if the lieutenant was aware that something was afoot. He didn't seem to be. She thought about what they were about to do and her jaw tightened.

She could hear him pouring water into the bedroom wash bowl and splashing his face. Then she heard the curtain rail creak. Perhaps he was getting suspicious – it was a good thing they had parked out of sight of the house.

She was there outside and smiled briskly as he appeared. 'Quick then,' she said, and tiptoed down the rickety stairs. They went out the back of the house to where a Citroën Traction Avant saloon was waiting. She opened the rear passenger door. Stearley got in and Natalie sat in the front.

'Hey, where's Harry?' he said.

Natalie turned round. 'Change of plan, Lieutenant. Best if you don't know.' She had rehearsed this line.

'But he's all right, isn't he?'

She nodded and said no more. It was impossible to see in the dark, but she sensed his unease, almost like an electrical current in the air.

They had brought Georges with them, a tough young man who would be quite able to handle the lieutenant if he got difficult. Next to Natalie in the driving seat was Jean-Pierre, her controller. She wondered how long it would take for Stearley to recognise him. He had gone to the Paris apartment and punched him in the gut after the incident with the German soldier.

She could feel herself getting angry even as she was reminded of it. She thought of her brother, Raymond, and her sister, Valérie, both murdered by the Gestapo. They held them for six weeks before they killed them. She was sure they had been tortured. Should she feel sorry for this *américain*? She could find a glimmer of pity. A lot of young people are foolish . . . but he should have known better, so she banished the thought from her head.

They drove on in silence. It really was dark outside. No stars, no moon, no lights in the distance. The blackout was total. Natalie hoped Jean-Pierre knew the road well, otherwise they were going to end up wrapped around a tree.

'So, where are we going?' Stearley asked again. He sounded rattled now.

Eventually Jean-Pierre spoke. 'We are taking you to another safe house.'

He said no more, but she could tell the lieutenant was getting more and more agitated. He was fidgeting and his breathing was increasingly loud.

Stearley spoke again. 'Look, if this is about me being a pain in the ass, then I'm sorry.'

Natalie spoke, trying to sound as matter-of-fact as she could. 'Really, monsieur, don't trouble yourself about it.'

Natalie exchanged a worried glance with Jean-Pierre, then noticed Stearley could see her in the rear-view mirror.

An awful silence descended.

They drove on a short while longer, then Jean-Pierre pulled the car over to the side of the road and stopped.

'Get out,' he snapped.

'Where's the safe house?' Stearley was close to panic now. They were in the middle of nowhere. 'Tell me what's going on.'

Georges had a gun; Natalie knew that. He would probably have to prod him in the ribs with it to get him out.

'Get out of the car,' Jean-Pierre said again.

Natalie was out now, standing by the side of the road. They were parked by a copse of tall poplars. There was some light from the moon now, and she could see Stearley was barely able to stand.

He turned to look back at Natalie, his eyes pleading, as if to say, 'Can't you get me out of this?'

There was a terrible pause. Stearley looked blank, then terrified. His mouth was moving but he seemed to have lost the power of speech. For a moment he struggled free of their grip, but Georges and Jean-Pierre quickly grabbed him and dragged him towards the dense woodland. She could see one of Georges's powerful hands clamped tight around Stearley's mouth.

Natalie could feel her legs beginning to tremble as she stood waiting by the car. Why was it taking so long?

Then she heard a single muffled shot.

A few minutes later Jean-Pierre and Georges returned, with Stearley's dog tags. No one would know what happened to him. He would be posted as 'missing, presumed dead'.

In the car she held back her tears. She didn't want Jean-Pierre and Georges to see she was upset. Before, she had been sure it had been the right thing to do. No one should be allowed to put the lives of the Resistance workers at risk like that. But now she felt remorse. Like them, the lieutenant was young, with his whole life ahead of him. The arrogance and folly of youth shouldn't be a death sentence. But these were terrible times.

CHAPTER 27

November 9th, 1943

Natalie woke Harry the next morning with the news that they would be travelling on to Bordeaux that day.

'I have the tickets and travel permits. We leave in half an hour.'

'I'll go wake the lieutenant,' he said.

Natalie shook her head. 'He's gone, Harry.'

'Gone? What do you mean?'

She wouldn't catch his eye. Then she said, 'We decided to separate you. He was too much trouble.'

'So what the hell's happened to him?'

'Lieutenant Stearley put our lives is danger. We warned him. He is on his own now,' she said coldly.

So it hadn't been an idle warning – the Resistance people had been true to their word. Harry didn't envy Stearley the task of finding his way through occupied France on his own. He might be in with a chance. His French was pretty good.

They caught the train to Bordeaux later that afternoon. Harry and Natalie sat in the same carriage but separately.

The journey was slow but uneventful and Natalie brought another newspaper for Harry to hide behind. This time it worked. No one engaged him in conversation. By midnight the whole carriage was asleep. Natalie had gone to sleep first.

The train reached Bordeaux at eight the next morning, and they disembarked with hundreds of other passengers. Ahead, at the platform end, they could see a great queue building, and many German soldiers. It seemed today was a day for a very thorough inspection of train tickets and travel permits.

Natalie seemed unperturbed and coolly walked into a platform-side café and Harry duly followed. She sat down at one end, and when he came in a few moments later she waved, calling him over in French. She ordered two coffees and indicated that Harry should 'read' his newspaper.

When the coffees arrived, Harry noticed a small key on her saucer. She pushed the scrap of paper to him. *Follow me into the corridor*, it read.

Harry nodded. He noticed a young Frenchman staring at them. He was joined a minute later by another man, who turned to look at them shortly after.

Natalie got up to go, but fortunately neither of the men across the café paid her any more attention. Harry followed soon after.

She was waiting in the corridor and quickly unlocked a side door next to the lavatories. It led straight out to an alley filled with dustbins, off a street running down the side of the station.

'The usual procedure, monsieur,' she whispered. They set off, Harry following Natalie at a discreet distance.

It took them an hour to reach their destination – an ordinary house in an outlying suburb. They were welcomed by a young man who seemed entirely pleased to see them. He spoke only French and left soon after they arrived.

'There are two guest rooms in the attic,' Natalie told Harry. 'We can go up there. If you hear any commotion, you'll have to hide as best you can. Now we eat, and then upstairs, yes?'

They were sitting in the dining room about to eat breakfast when the phone in the corner rang. Harry nearly jumped out of his skin. Natalie rushed to answer it. She turned pale and her rapidly spoken words finished abruptly – mid-sentence. She stood looking at the receiver aghast.

'We have to go. Immediately,' she said.

'What's wrong?' Harry said.

Natalie shook her head. 'This place is not safe.'

They grabbed bags and left without so much as picking up any food from the table.

'Whatever happens, don't run. Nothing attracts suspicion like a running man,' she said. She walked close to Harry, arm in arm as if they were lovers for a few brief steps, and spoke under her breath. 'There's another safe

236

house out in Pessac. It's on the edge of town. We can get there in maybe an hour if we walk fast. I'll walk ahead. You keep up.'

Still walking together, wrapped up in the confusion of what had just happened, they turned a corner. Right ahead was a German roadblock. There were a few cars and a waiting crowd. Harry could already see a German soldier looking straight over at them. It was too late to turn round, and definitely too late to pretend that they weren't together. 'Keep walking,' she whispered softly, her arm still in his. 'We're going to have to go through this.'

The soldier beckoned for them to stand with a group of people selected to have their passes scrutinised in detail, while others were waved through. Harry felt his heart pounding in his chest. What if they started to speak to him? What if they asked him anything that wasn't written on that identity card?

Two officers were sitting in a staff car by the roadblock and were staring directly at him with undisguised hostility. They wore the insignia of the SS. Maybe they thought he looked like a Jew? He could feel his legs start to shake and realised he was beginning to sweat. He might as well have *I AM AN AMERICAN JEW* stamped on a placard around his neck.

He glanced over to Natalie, who looked as calm and collected as ever.

Salvation came from an unexpected quarter. Air-raid sirens started up and the German guard told them that the nearest shelter was three streets away and that all pedestrians should hurry there at once.

Almost immediately the bombs started to fall – far away but enough to feel the blast in their ears. Harry looked up to see wave after wave of bombers almost overhead and coming in over the west, tiny flecks in the blue sky, with their wispy white contrails.

A series of explosions came nearer and nearer, close enough now to make the earth tremble beneath their feet. A woman screamed and several dogs began to bark loudly. In the stillness after the first bomb detonations they could hear the steady buzz of aero-engines and the slow cascade of a collapsing building.

They reached the shelter and hurried down its concrete steps. Natalie banged hard on the metal door. There were at least twenty desperate people behind them, pushing down the stairs. Harry felt the life being squeezed out of him. He was crushed against the door and could barely breathe. There were further explosions, seemingly just down the street, the blasts turning them momentarily deaf. People were screaming and the crowd seemed close to panic.

Natalie banged again on the door and shouted angrily at the top of her voice. Harry could barely believe she had the breath or strength to do it. But the door opened and there was a mad stampede inside. She pushed her way determinedly through the packed bodies in the shelter and Harry followed right behind. Some cursed but she apologised sweetly.

There was space in the far corner of the shelter, but it was lit by the gloomiest of little bulbs and the smell was deeply unpleasant. They sat down to regain their breath.

A steady pattern of explosions brought Harry back to reality. They were creeping nearer all the time. Those sticks of bombs that fell from a Fortress – he'd never really thought about what happened when they hit the ground. Bortz usually dropped them in series rather than all at once. Their Fortress flew at about 250 miles an hour over a bomb drop, so it seemed logical that those twelve bombs in the bomb bay would come down a second or two apart in almost a straight line. Now here he was directly underneath them, counting those explosions as they fell overhead.

The shelter lights flickered and they were plunged into darkness. But the lights came back on after a moment, casting their grudging glow over pale, frightened faces. Most of the people in here were women, with a smattering of older men. The rest, the children and the men, must be sheltering at work or in their schools.

Harry was surprised the sirens had gone off so late before the raid began. He'd always told himself they would get plenty of warning down below. But maybe the French weren't expecting a raid on their city. Maybe they had thought the bomber stream was heading over to one of the industrial cities in northern Italy? Either way, he felt bad his own people were bombing a conquered nation. Then he felt doubly anxious. If anyone discovered they had a real-life American in their midst, they might want to lynch him.

The all-clear sounded soon after that.

'Follow me,' whispered Natalie in his ear. 'Don't lose me.'

They hurried down the street and it was difficult for Harry to keep her in sight with all the streams of citizens pouring out of shelters. Like everyone around him, Harry felt disoriented. Something utterly unnatural had happened, a catastrophe of biblical proportions. The people on the ground had been visited by a vengeful monster and evidence of its rage was all around. There was an awful smell of black smoke, and drains and gas, accompanied by the sounds of wailing and lamentation. Certainly everyone around him looked terribly anxious. They were probably wondering if they still had homes to go to and if their loved ones, away in school or at the factories or dockyard, were still alive.

Harry could still see Natalie, ahead in the crowd. Every now and then she would stop and tie a shoelace or rummage in her bag. After a while he realised she was doing this whenever she thought he was lagging too far behind. He quickened his pace and wondered what other horrors the day would hold.

CHAPTER 28

They sat together on a bench in a small park on the edge of town to rest. There was no one else in the park and they were free to speak in hushed tones.

'Why would we bomb Bordeaux?' he said, as much to himself as to her.

'Docks, factories . . . the usual reason you bomb anything.' She sounded distant, distracted. She didn't seem angry, just forlorn. Harry could see she was upset.

'Forgive me, monsieur,' she said, blinking away a tear from her eye. 'This morning, it was bad news . . .'

'Can you tell me what happened?'

'Jean-Pierre, he . . . was my controller. He is the man who came to the apartment in Paris.'

Harry remembered him.

'They shot him while he was talking to me on the phone this morning.' She wiped away another tear.

Harry was appalled and did not really know what to say.

'He had just enough time to tell me their house had been raided. Then they shot him.'

241

'Did you think they would be coming for you too? Is that why we had to go immediately?' asked Harry.

She nodded. 'They know about that house where Jean-Pierre was,' she said, 'so they probably know about the safe house where we were hiding too. Someone betrayed us. And I think I know who it was.' Then her face hardened. 'I will kill him.'

Harry didn't doubt it.

They sat in silence while she composed herself.

'So won't they know about the place where we're going to?' said Harry.

Natalie shook her head firmly. 'Trust me. The English have a funny little expression,' she said. 'Belt and braces. You understand?'

Harry looked blankly at her.

'Well, the house we've just been in is the belt. Now I will take you to the braces.'

Harry felt utterly puzzled but shrugged and decided to wait and see what would happen next.

They walked on, separate but in sight, stopping only to drink water straight from a fountain. The dust and smoke from the raid still hung in the air and created a terrible thirst.

After another half an hour of trudging around the outer suburbs of Bordeaux, Harry saw Natalie stop at a modern house. She knocked at the door and entered. Harry waited outside, hoping no one would come along and ask him what he thought he was doing, skulking around the neighbourhood.

Five minutes later she came out, looked around and walked along a narrow path at the side of the house. Harry took that as his cue to follow. She caught his eye and with the smallest gesture beckoned him into the garden.

Here a stout-looking woman in her fifties ushered them both through the garden thick with untended vegetation to where concrete stairs led down to a cellar door.

The room was pitch black but there was shuffling, there was breathing and there was an unmistakable smell of unwashed humans and unwashed clothes. Harry went to light a match and as he struck sparks on the rough striking board an unmistakably English voice said, 'Careful there. The stink down here is probably inflammable!' There was a sniggering from somewhere else. As the match head blazed into flame he and Natalie found themselves surrounded by four dishevelled-looking men, all with several days' growth of beard. They introduced themselves in the time it took for the flame to burn to Harry's fingers. Two of them were English, two American.

'This calls for the candle, I think,' said one of the Englishmen. A small stub was lit and cast a dull glow around the cellar. 'Can't have it on for long, not for now anyway – we're almost running out.'

All of the men looked at Natalie with surprise. 'Well, bonjour, mademoiselle,' said the younger Englishman.

The others smiled and nodded. The English airmen introduced themselves as Colin and Geoffrey.

One of the Americans was much older than the rest of
them, serious and aloof, and lost no time telling them he
was a colonel, and Harry instinctively saluted him.

'Knock it off,' he said curtly. 'We're done with that for
now.' His demeanour didn't invite further conversation.

The other American was in his thirties and introduced
himself as Walter. He was friendly and told them they'd
been cooped up in the cellar for three days, mostly in darkness, since they could only light their candle when they ate.
They were all bored to distraction and desperate to move
on to a more comfortable hiding place. Anywhere, really,
where you could see. Harry sensed that he and Natalie were
a welcome distraction.

The Limeys were RAF guys – Lancaster crew – a radio op
and bomb aimer from the same 'kite', they called it, which
had come down close to Amiens, on the way back from
Saarbrücken.

'So are these people who are hiding us OK?' asked
Harry.

'They keep us cooped up in here,' said Geoffrey. 'It's
been three days now, and you can barely see your pot to
piss in – beg your pardon, mademoiselle – but the food's
good, first rate.'

'We came mainly by train,' said Harry, keen to distract
himself. 'So it's been fairly rapid progress.' Natalie kicked
him hard.

'Lucky you,' said Colin. 'We've been on bicycles for most of our trip. At night too. It's been a right old pantomime. Can't tell you how many times I've landed arse over tit when the bike hit a pothole.'

The candle flickered in its holder. 'Better blow that out,' said Walter. 'We can talk in the dark.'

But they didn't talk. Conversation petered out and soon the room was filled with the sound of snoring. There was little else to do but sleep.

Sometime that afternoon there was a noise at the top of the stairs. Harry woke with a start but relaxed when he saw the silhouette of the French woman who had met them in the garden. Natalie went to talk to her, then came down to translate what had been said.

'The British gentlemen, you will go now with the colonel in a lorry with sheep and fodder for a farm close to the border. If you are lucky, you will be there late this afternoon.'

The British airmen went with heartfelt goodbyes, the colonel with a surly nod.

'The colonel is in pretty hot water if he makes it back,' Walter said after he'd gone. 'He's a real hero in my eyes. He told us his division commander had refused him permission to fly. Anyone who goes out over Germany with his men when he clearly doesn't have to is one brave son of a bitch.'

Harry nodded. 'I liked those British guys,' he said. 'They were lively company.'

'Yeah, I'm sorry to see them go,' said Walter. 'You know, both those guys are wounded, but you don't hear them complaining about it. That takes guts.'

As they sat there in the dark, Harry was consumed with thoughts of his dead friends. His final moments with John Hill ran through his mind, as if on a loop. He felt especially sad that he would never have the chance to meet John and his family back home in New York, and he resolved that he would look his parents up if he managed to get through this. Even when he dozed he would wake with a start, having dreamed he was back aboard his doomed Fortress, hearing machine-gun fire and not being able to see where it came from.

That evening, their host bought them a bean cassoulet and a carafe of red wine. She also announced she had a new candle, but this too needed to be used very carefully.

So they ate and drank by candlelight and then snuffed the flame out.

This time they did talk. Mainly about what they were going to do when they got home, although Natalie said not a word.

Walter said he was longing to see his family in Chicago. He hadn't been home since February 1942. He had two little daughters he barely knew, the youngest being born just a month before he shipped out. Harry was keen to know what he was doing before he was shot down. 'We flew Liberators out of Halesworth,' he said. 'But hey, I'm with your French girl. Careless talk and all that.'

Harry spent a restless night, tormented by the same dreams that had visited him during the afternoon. In his moments of wakefulness, his thoughts turned to Stearley. He wondered if he was sleeping in a hedgerow somewhere. Without Natalie his chances were almost non-existent, he realised now.

Harry could hear Natalie breathing and knew she was still awake. But he didn't speak for fear of disturbing Walter. It was awful being cooped up in the dark, but at least he was still free and still alive.

CHAPTER 29

Bordeaux, November 11th, 1943

They were roused early by the French couple who were hiding them. The woman talked rapidly to Natalie, and from the look of relief on her face Harry thought there would be good news.

'Madame says we are going today,' Natalie told them. 'Walter, you will come with us. We go on bicycles as soon as it gets dark. Madame says she will bring a good breakfast for us all shortly.' She said that they should sleep that day as they would be cycling all night. This final leg, Bordeaux to Bayonne, would take three or four days by bicycle, and then they would be on foot. Over the mountains and into Spain.

'That will be the most difficult part of your journey,' she said. She gave a brief, encouraging nod. 'But it is exciting, yes? You are almost there.'

Harry wondered how many times she had accompanied Allied servicemen escaping on this route before. He knew so little about her, but admired her courage and how someone so young could put her life in so much danger for strangers. He dozed on and off throughout the daylight hours and they were all asleep when their host arrived with fresh clothes and a thick lentil broth. They were directed up the stairs and Harry could see at once it was dark outside.

Before they left, Madame gave Harry a present – a black beret. She talked rapidly to Natalie, who said it was to hide Harry's dark hair. The dye had worn off now and his own black roots were showing through.

A tall young man with wire glasses, barely more than twenty, was waiting for them outside the house. Harry guessed he was a student. Four bicycles stood against the wall. He spoke to Natalie and she turned to Harry and Walter to explain that he would be accompanying them down to the border and that they should maintain complete silence at all times. He would lead and it was imperative that they all keep up with each other. He would stay far enough ahead of them so if they were stopped it would not be obvious that he was travelling with them. If there was any sign of a patrol or even other passengers on the road, they should stop and hide. There was no curfew in this region of France, but being out at that time would still be regarded with suspicion. He was sure, continued Natalie, that there would be very few people out and about on the roads they would be taking.

The next few days passed in a blur. By night they cycled in almost pitch darkness beneath overcast skies. But a strong tailwind helped them keep a good speed and when they reached each day's safe house close to dawn they would collapse in exhaustion and sleep until mid-afternoon. Their guide was so aloof they did not even know his name, and the people who helped shelter them were similarly detached. Natalie said there had been several breaches in security recently and scores of arrests. It was much more difficult to find people willing to help the Resistance now. Harry thought it was no wonder that everywhere they stopped they were treated with suspicion.

But Harry was so exhausted by these night rides that he didn't care. As long as he had a bed for the night, and something to put in his belly, that was all that mattered.

'We must be close to the border by now, right?' Walter asked Natalie on their second night, as they prepared to bed down on bare boards up in a dusty attic. 'You know what this town is called?'

Natalie didn't say the name, just that there would be a final stop before they tackled the mountainous border. Harry marvelled at how she maintained her guard, even with them. But he realised she was right not to say anything. He remembered Tilly's joking complaints about 'Careless talk costs lives', but here in occupied France this was a deadly serious business. Harry knew in his heart that if he was captured and tortured as a spy, there was nothing that he wouldn't confess.

He tried to settle, and fiddled nervously with his dog tags as he waited to fall asleep. He wanted to throw those wretched tin tabs away – they had an 'H' for Hebrew stamped on them. So the first thing the Krauts would find out, when they captured him, was that he was a Jew. But he also remembered the warnings they had been given back in Kirkstead, about airmen without dog tags being shot as spies. On balance he supposed it was better to keep them.

Natalie, lying next to him, was a restless sleeper. She tossed and turned and had frequent nightmares that made her whimper in her sleep. But he was still afraid of that terrible carapace she had. How would she ever let that go when the war was over?

It seemed as if he had just drifted off to sleep when Natalie gently shook his shoulder. 'Come on, our guide's here,' she told him.

Their host, an elderly Frenchman with a snow-white beard, introduced them to a short, wiry man with brown leathery skin. There was something almost animal-like about him and it was obvious he had spent a lifetime in the mountains.

He shook their hands and told them his name was Miquel.

'Hey, *les américains*,' he said, shaking Harry and Walter by the hand. He looked doubtfully at their light clothes. 'The mountains, they are cold at this time. But you look tough, eh! Wear everything clothing, and if we are lucky, we get there in a day!'

Walter surprised them all by producing a little camera he had been carrying in his rucksack. 'Can I have a picture?' he asked. Everyone looked alarmed, especially the old man who was hiding them.

Walter backtracked, holding up his hands. 'This is the most exciting adventure of my life,' he explained. 'I wasn't thinking. I just want something to show to my girls when I get back to Chicago.'

Miquel gave him a generous smile, the white of his teeth glowing against his dark brown skin. He spoke to Natalie in French. She didn't translate, but Harry knew she would never agree to them being photographed.

It was a frosty bright night, not ideal for travelling, but Miquel explained there was snow on the way, maybe over the next twenty-four hours, and once that came down it would make the crossing almost impossible. Quite apart from the danger and the cold, snow meant footprints. It was too easy to be followed. They had to go now.

When they got up to leave, Natalie announced she would not be coming with them. 'Miquel will take you to the border and help you get to the British Consulate in Bilbao. There the British will arrange for you to travel back to England.'

Harry knew at once he would never see her again. Much to his surprise, he felt like crying.

'Thank you for everything,' he said.

She could see he was upset and came over and hugged him tightly. 'You've been so brave, Harry,' she said. 'I have been lucky to travel with you.' She kissed him on both cheeks, and wiped a tear away with her finger.

Harry watched her cycle away into the dark with the young man who had accompanied them. Having wondered how Natalie would be if she survived the war, he had been moved by her sudden display of tenderness and knew she would be all right. Seeing her gentler side made him realise she had a kind of bravery he could only begin to imagine.

They moved as quickly and silently as they could. At any moment they might hear a challenge or the sound of a rifle being cocked, or even fired. It was awful living like this, thought Harry. He felt permanently tense. It was even worse than flying. At least with a Fortress you could see your enemy coming and you knew when you needed to be frightened and when it was OK to relax.

Miquel led them into a pine forest and kept a few feet ahead. The moonlight was a mixed blessing. Their little group would be easily spotted, but at least they could make out the guide's silhouette and the way ahead.

Harry could feel his legs beginning to tire, and no wonder – the path through the forest was on an increasingly steep slope. Walter walked ahead with their guide, and then hung back to wait for Harry to catch up.

'He says we're taking the long way round here,' he told him. 'Miquel knows where the guard posts are but it's the patrols we have to be especially careful about.'

The forest came to an abrupt end and all at once they were climbing a vertiginous slope of slippery scree and Harry found himself gasping for air, his breath glowing in the moonlight.

The path narrowed and Harry could see they were going through a pass with a steep rock face on either side.

'We have to hurry through here,' said Miquel. 'If we're spotted by a patrol, we'll be picked off with ease. There's nowhere to hide.'

It was the longest twenty minutes of Harry's life. As they scrambled up the great boulders that filled the steep gully, all he could hear was the scraping of boots on rock and the sound of his own breathing. He was drenched in cold sweat and felt chilled to the bone in spite of the exertion. At once he had a flashback to his turret in the *Macey May*.

Eventually the steep rock sides curved out and they appeared to have reached a plateau. Harry was beginning to wonder how much longer he could carry on. Walter patted him on the back – 'Well done, Sergeant!'

He beamed. 'Jesus, I'm shattered.'

Miquel picked this moment to tell them they were going to stop in a small cave for some rest. It was only another few minutes away.

The cave was dank and had a horrible smell about it. Harry wondered if something had died in there. Miquel led them on into the gloom, and when they were so far inside they could barely see, he took out a small flashlight and shone it ahead.

'Quick, to build a fire,' said Miquel.

He indicated they would light the fire at the very end and said they should all look for twigs and small branches. Harry thought that was a great idea. If he didn't warm up soon, he might just curl up in a ball and die of exposure.

They went off to find wood, no one venturing too far from the others. As Harry bent to pick up a twig, he heard a guttural growl and found himself staring straight into the eyes of a bear. He was close enough to smell its stinking breath and see the saliva glisten in its jaws. It might not have been that large, but it looked ferocious and ready to attack.

Harry froze, and suddenly Walter charged towards the animal, snarling angrily and brandishing a hefty branch. The bear turned and fled.

As Harry sat flabbergasted on the ground, Walter let out a laugh. 'Got to show these creatures who's boss,' he chuckled, and offered a hand to help Harry stand.

Ten minutes later Miquel had built a fire in the deepest part of the cave. Harry felt his strength returning as the flames warmed him and he ate the bread and cheese they had been given for the journey. 'Two hours we rest,' declared Miquel. 'Then we walk more.'

It was difficult to sleep – the ground was too lumpy and it was too cold – but Harry was glad of the rest. Miquel managed to sleep though; Harry could hear him snoring.

They carried on before first light the next morning, listening in the silence beyond their footfalls for anything that would suggest anyone was stalking them.

After an eternity, a pale rim of light appeared on the horizon and darkness receded.

Harry was freezing to death and could no longer feel his toes in his boots. His eyes were streaming with the cold and he wondered if he was going to get frostbite. But the view was breathtaking.

'Look at the sunrise,' said Walter. It was magical. They were above the clouds and the rising sun was lighting them from below. Harry thought sadly of his brother and the hiking weekends they had spent in the Catskill Mountains, north of New York. This was the sort of view David would have talked about for weeks. Harry wondered how there could be such beauty in such a frightening world.

Miquel spoke to them both. 'Down there, we reach the big river. Then border post. Come.'

He pressed on. Now they were walking downhill and nearing the final part of their journey.

CHAPTER 30

The Pyrenees, November 19th, 1943

When it got fully light, Harry expected them to hide and rest but Miquel had no such plan. He explained that they needed to press on as quickly as they could. The sky was heavy with dark clouds that promised snow. They needed to get down past the border post before it started to fall.

They trudged on, stopping briefly when Miquel told them it was noon. For a few moments, a watery sun emerged from behind low dark cloud. Even this momentary glimpse was enough to warm their spirits. Walter smiled, and as they ate the last of their rations he shared his cheese with Harry.

'We will soon reach the river near the border,' said Miquel. The plan was to keep hidden in the tall trees along the bank and walk north towards a rope bridge. The river would be too dangerous to cross in any other way.

'Now, very important,' Miquel continued. 'In Spain, they don't like *les américains*. The border guard sees us, maybe he shoot to kill.' Natalie had briefed them earlier on the dangers they would face in Spain. If they were caught, the Spanish authorities would send Miquel back to

France to face the Gestapo. Harry and Walter could be interned in a camp. They would not be safe until they reached the British consulate in Bilbao.

An hour later, Harry heard the sound of roaring water and knew at once why they would have to cross by bridge. His feet hurt and his hands were freezing, but he kept quiet.

The river was every bit as frightening as Harry expected. It was not as wide as he had feared, narrow enough in fact to throw a stone from one bank to the other, but water poured down from the mountains feeding a great torrent that would sweep away anyone foolish enough to try to ford it.

As the afternoon wore on, flakes of snow occasionally fell from the sky, but never settled to a steady flow. Shortly before dark Miquel turned to them both and put a finger to his pursed lips. 'Ten minute,' he said. 'Border post.'

They crept forward, conscious of each snapped twig and brushed leaf. As the twilight settled, a fog rose and shrouded the landscape. It settled on the little group, adding an extra layer of damp misery to their exhausted bodies.

After half an hour Harry could see a pinprick of light on the far side. He tapped Miquel on the shoulder and pointed to it. Miquel slapped him on the back and whispered that they should all be extra quiet.

Soon after, they saw the bridge emerge from the mist – a spindly rope construction with wooden slats. Harry couldn't believe it. It was the sort of thing explorers crossed in

Saturday morning B-movies. They were usually clutching Inca treasure and pursued by angry, spear-waving natives. In the movies, bridges like this were always rickety and crumbled when you stepped on them, but this bridge had been recently creosoted, and the wood was polished and sturdy. He allowed himself a little chuckle. They had been lucky so far in their border crossing. All they had had to put up with was a brief altercation with a bear.

Miquel called them together and they huddled close so as to hear him over the roar of the river. He pointed to a small wooden shed on the far side. 'We wait. They sleep, we go. OK?'

It seemed a simple enough plan. But the wait was interminable. And while they lay there on the frozen ground the snow began to fall in earnest. Within minutes it lay over every surface.

The light in the guards' hut eventually flickered out. Walter kept getting up to go to the bridge, but Miquel held him back. 'We wait . . . until they sleep for sure,' he had to keep saying.

Eventually, when Harry was so cold he thought he would never be able to move his fingers again, Miquel stood up. 'Very quietly. You have to go under the window, yes?' He modelled crouching down to walk – at all costs they must not disturb the men inside.

'Walter first, then Harry, then me. OK!'

Walter crossed the snow-covered bridge in a bare minute. If it creaked, then the roar of the river drowned out the noise. They saw his silhouette crouch down and crawl past the hut, exactly as instructed.

Now it was Harry's turn. He screwed his eyes up so he could barely see the river below him and began to make his way across. The snow on the polished wood and the swaying of the bridge as it moved under his weight were a treacherous combination, and three-quarters of the way over he slipped on the icy slats. He frantically grabbed at the side of the bridge as he tried to regain his balance but he toppled over, almost falling through the gaps between the ropes, and for a moment he dangled over the void. In a flash Miquel was up on the bridge and helping him to his feet.

He said nothing but his eyes spoke for him: *What the hell are you doing?*

Once they were both back on the bridge, Miquel beckoned for Harry to continue. Harry's feet touched Spanish soil. At once he was reminded of the moment his feet touched the ground when he'd parachuted out of the *Macey May*. He wanted to shout out loud in triumph. Now he no longer had to worry about the Gestapo. But he stayed silent. With a huge grin on his face he crept past the shed. Inside he could hear a man snoring so loud you could easily hear him despite the roaring river.

Miquel arrived over at the trees a few moments later. 'What next?' said Harry. He felt he could walk another ten, twenty miles, no problem.

Then he noticed Walter had stood to one side and was pointing a pistol at them.

CHAPTER 31

'Out, out in the open.' He was shouting at them now. Harry looked at him in amazement, but Walter shook his head contemptuously. 'You dumb louse. Now, all of you, put your bags down and your hands clear in the air. Anyone makes any trouble, I'll shoot you without a second thought.'

To make his point, he let off his pistol and the shot thudded into the ground just in front of Harry's left foot.

'*¡Eh! amigos! ¡Venga y ayúdeme!*' he bellowed at the top of his voice. Harry's sense of impending catastrophe deepened. Who was this guy? Was he in league with the border guards? Who would have guessed he spoke Spanish?

Nothing happened. Walter called out again. This time, after a pause, the light inside the shed came on.

'Come on,' Walter indicated with his pistol. 'Get over there.'

A door opened and a sleepy man, dressed in the uniform of the Spanish National Guard, stumbled out.

He too was armed. Now Harry and Miquel had two guns pointing at them.

Walter spoke to the guard in Spanish and then pushed his captives inside the border post. Harry heard Walter use the word *teléfono* several times, but the guard shrugged. They didn't have one. Under the watchful eye of the guard, Harry and Miquel were each tied to a chair with twine.

'Have a rest, boys,' said Walter to his captives. He was enjoying mocking them. 'We're all going to be busy when the relief guards arrive in the morning.'

They sat in the glow of a gas lamp, the captives down one end of the room, Walter and the guard at the other, guns raised. Harry's heart was beating fast. This was the end of the road. Maybe he would spend the rest of the war in a Spanish concentration camp; he hoped Natalie had been right and they would not send him back to the Nazis in France. But he felt sick with anxiety for Miquel. It was difficult to tell in the low light, but his guide looked white with fear. The thought of Miquel being tortured and then executed filled Harry with horror. Anger boiled up inside him.

'What's your game, Walter?' he shouted. 'Are you some kind of nut?'

Walter gave a smug smirk. 'You suckers,' he laughed. 'You let me follow you all the way down the escape line from Amiens. Those Resistance bastards won't know what hit them when I get to talk to the Gestapo. Paris, Bordeaux . . .' He turned to Miquel. 'And you creeps in your piss-ant border town.' He looked at the Spanish guard.

'At least Pedro here has been doing his job properly. We thought the border guards might be open to bribes.'

Anger flashed in Walter's eyes. 'We're on the wrong side,' he said. 'We should have listened to the German American Bund before we got involved with the Limeys. With our Jewish press, pumping out their hate for Hitler, America didn't stand a chance. I knew I did the right thing when I came over here to fight with Franco in the Spanish Civil War. Then I went with the fascists to fight over in Russia as part of the Blue Division. Bolshevism has to be stopped before it takes over the world. And their pals, the lousy Jews. They're just dupes for the Jews back home.'

'So what the hell are you doing here?' asked Harry.

'They asked me to infiltrate the escape lines. Gave me an airman outfit, dog tags, the lot. You all bought that story about Chicago and the girl, didn't you? I wouldn't live in that mongrel nation again. Not now I know how a good fascist country can be run.'

Now he'd started, Walter didn't feel like stopping. He'd played a role these last few days and now he could be himself. He turned on Harry.

'You just came over from England, didn't you? I hear the Limeys let the Blacks over there run free – dating those English girls. They have the right idea in Germany. Girls who consort with subhumans get sent to concentration camps.'

'The Germans are gonna lose this war,' said Harry with conviction. 'And when they do, you're gonna be shot as a traitor.'

Walter laughed cruelly, then came over to Harry and pulled his head back by yanking on his hair. 'You look like a Yid. I knew you were a Jew boy the minute I saw you. Maybe I'll shoot you. They're not so intent on cleansing their Jews this side of the border. Don't give me any excuses.' Then he picked up a bayonet lying on the table and tapped his finger on the tip of the blade. 'Or maybe I'll just slit your throat . . .'

Miquel spoke up. 'You will never win after Stalingrad. Soon the Americans will come, and the British and the Canadians. They will come over the sea. They will take back *la France*. And their bombers will reduce your Third Reich to dust.'

'Hey, mountain man, I'd shoot you with pleasure. But I'm sure our Gestapo friends will enjoy hearing what you have to say. Maybe you'll tell them about your pretty little French girl. She's clever. It's a shame she's on the wrong side too. The Germans will make a real mess out of her when they catch up with our Natalie.' His eyes hardened. 'Stalingrad was just a temporary setback. This is a turning point in world history. National Socialism will disinfect the diseases of Bolshevism and Capitalism. Yes, the invasion will come from the west and it'll be destroyed on the beaches. I've fought side by side with German soldiers. And they're the best in the world.

'Now excuse me, gentlemen, but much as I'm enjoying our little conversation, I need to piss.' He turned to the guard and said, '*Tengo que mear,*' then walked outside.

The guard looked at the two of them and, much to their surprise, winked. He got up, picked up his rifle and walked out too. A moment later a shot rang out.

The guard returned. They looked on, astonishment etched across their faces. He picked up the bayonet and for a moment Harry wondered if he was going to kill them too. But he didn't. He knelt down behind each of them and cut them free.

'I live in America for two years.' He spoke in heavily accented English as he sawed at Harry's bonds. 'I like your "Mongrel" Nation.' Then he said, 'And my name is Luis, not Pedro.'

He spoke to Miquel in French. '*Vous êtes deux veinards . . .*' Miquel chuckled as Luis continued to speak, then explained to Harry. 'We are two lucky bastards. The guard who is usually here with him tonight is a hundred per cent Franco fascist and he loves the Nazis.'

They went outside to where Walter was lying face down on the ground, the back of his head a bloody pulp. It was a good thing that Walter had gone outside; it would have made a terrible mess in the guard hut. The guard gave his body a hefty kick. He was dead all right.

Harry and Miquel picked him up by the legs, and the guard held on to his arms. They stood beside of the river and swung him back and forth three times before hurling him into the water.

'Thank you for helping us,' Harry said as they walked back to the hut.

'Two of my brothers, they joined the Blue Division,' said the guard, 'The one that jerk talk about. Both killed in the siege of Leningrad. My poor mother. Died of a broken heart.' He crossed himself.

Harry was confused. 'But Spain isn't fighting in the war?' he said.

'Blue Division is volunteers – all Spanish soldiers, fighting Soviets.' He sighed. 'We back the wrong side of this war, my friends . . . Now, inside. I make coffee.'

Miquel and the guard spoke for a while in French. Miquel told Harry, 'Luis here will look after you.' The next guard shift was due to arrive at six o'clock and they mustn't know anything, so Harry would have to hide in the woods. 'I'll stay *un moment*, then I go back through the mountains.'

They drank their sweet black coffee in a daze. Harry felt a huge debt of gratitude to Miquel. When he got up to go, he gave Harry a handshake and a hug that almost crushed the life out of him. '*Bonne chance!*' he said. Then he vanished over the bridge.

The guard gave Harry a thick greatcoat hanging up behind the door. He told Harry to walk to the road, a kilometre or two to the east, where there was shelter by roadside. When his shift was finished, Luis would meet him there and take him on to Bilbao.

CHAPTER 32

December 18th, 1943

Luis had driven Harry to Bilbao and dropped him a street away from the British consulate. From here arrangements had been made to have him returned by boat to England. Four weeks later he found himself at the main entrance to Kirkstead Air Base, just as dusk was falling.

It seemed unreal. He had made it back for the week before Christmas. And, as the carol promised, the snow lay crisp and even over the base and the flat fields of Norfolk. Snow did wonderful things to any landscape, even the muddy and dreary Nissen huts of Kirkstead. Everything looked so beautiful in the late afternoon light.

He was eighteen now, his October birthday literally forgotten in the strange blurred weeks of his escape. In his heart he knew he was no longer the boy who had arrived here on that late summer's day. Now he was back he felt like a hardened veteran.

As he walked towards the main ops room to report his arrival, he was surrounded by unfamiliar faces. What was it someone had said one night in the canteen? 'You don't see dead bodies in this job, just empty beds.' He had seen both now.

His thoughts quickly turned to the rest of his crew. John, especially, was never far from his thoughts. One of the first things he had promised to do when he got back was to write to his friend's family, and his girl, Shirley. Then he thought of Corrales, and how much the lanky tail gunner had made him laugh, and the other guys he knew for sure were dead – Holberg, Dalinsky, Skaggs, Cain . . . He hadn't liked them all, but they still felt like brothers. They had been through a lot together. He felt his throat close up and his chest grow heavy. Back in Kirkstead his dead companions surrounded him like gossamer spectres.

A hearty shout jolted him back to the real world. 'Haaarrrrryyyy!!!!' It was Ernie Benik, who let out a great whoop of triumph. 'Hey, fellas,' he cried, 'Friedman's back!'

The other ground crew ran over to greet him, and Harry found himself borne up on their shoulders. Complete strangers joined in and the crowd around him grew to a swirling multitude. This was what Frank Sinatra must feel like when he was mobbed by bobby-soxers. Even Colonel Kittering emerged from the control tower to see what the fuss was about.

As the colonel approached, the mob grew subdued and everyone stood to attention.

'It's Sergeant Friedman, sir,' said Ernie Benik. 'From the *Macey May*.'

'Goddamn it! We thought you were dead!' Kittering cried. 'Come and have a whiskey.'

Kittering took him into his office and poured a drink from a crystal decanter. Harry didn't like whiskey but he took a gulp and swallowed the fiery liquid anyway. Again, he was flushed with a feeling of relief. He had made it home.

'So, tell me all about it, son,' said Kittering.

Harry told the colonel about the Resistance and his escape across France, who had died in the *Macey May* and how Holberg had sacrificed his life, holding the bomber steady while the rest of the crew had tried to escape.

Harry thought he had lost him when he talked about the crew. He realised the colonel spent his life hearing about men under his command who had died, and he could barely remember one from the other.

'Friedman, I'm going to recommend you for a Distinguished Flying Cross,' said the colonel. Then he turned serious. 'Sergeant, we sent your kit back home. We posted you as missing, presumed dead. Look, we gotta get a telegram out to your mom and dad as soon as possible.'

Heart in mouth, Harry asked a question that had been haunting him ever since he arrived back in England. 'So, sir, do I get assigned to a new crew?'

The colonel shook his head. 'No, you're off active duty. We never let downed airmen back over Europe. If you got shot down again, there'd be too much the Gestapo could torture out of you about all the people who helped you.

We'll send you back Stateside for compassionate leave, then you can stay there and train the new boys, or you can come back and train them here. You can make up your own mind, but I'd like you back here. It does the men good to see a flyer who came back.

'And you'll be in good company. I've got a surprise for you.' Kittering stood up and called for his secretary. A young woman in Women's Army Corps uniform appeared at the door. 'Get this young man a coffee, Alice, and find him his mail. And have the major come straight over when his briefing is finished.'

Harry sat next to a warm stove and read through a handful of letters – two from his mom and dad, which stopped abruptly in the middle of October, when they would have heard he was missing. There was one from his cousin in New Jersey, and one without a stamp that had been hand-delivered. He guessed at once who had sent it, and he was right.

Tilly told him she had turned up at the dance and had been shocked to hear he had not returned from the raid – though they wouldn't tell her where it was. She told him she had gone home that night and cried. Now she was writing, as an act of faith, as she was certain he would return, and when he did she wanted him to send a note so she would know he was back. 'I've met quite a few of you boys from the base, but none of them have been like you.'

As he folded her letter, he thought he would ask for permission to go and see her as soon as possible.

There was a brief knock at the door and Harry looked up to see a familiar face. There in front of him was Bob Holberg.

The two hugged like long-lost brothers. 'Harry! I was sure you were dead. I quit the plane just a second before she started to cartwheel.'

'She broke up on the way down,' said Harry. 'Stearley got out too. Is he back yet?'

Holberg shook his head. 'No word. I hope he's OK. He's probably found himself a cute little mademoiselle and is laying low for a while.'

'What about the others?' asked Harry, half dreading the reply he would receive.

'Red Cross tell us LaFitte is in a camp in Saxony,' said Holberg. 'He's pretty badly wounded, we're told. They're trying to get him repatriated. There's no news of Bortz.'

That made Harry feel uneasy. Bortz had bailed out. Maybe they'd caught him and singled him out for special treatment because he was Jewish.

'And you?' asked Harry. 'How did you get back?'

Holberg laughed. 'Hooked up with the Resistance and they sent me back over the Channel. When you've unpacked your bags I'm taking you out for a drink and I'll tell you all about it.

'You know you're off active service now?' asked Holberg.

'Yes.'

'Come back here after your leave, Harry,' said Holberg. 'We need people like you and me around the base. Those guys that are flying combat missions – they need reminding that they can survive the war.'

Harry thought of Tilly and her note. He smiled and nodded. 'I'm coming back.'

Then he asked, 'Captain, who do I ask for an evening pass out of the base?'

Holberg laughed. 'I'm a major now – I can write you an evening pass.'

Harry hurried down the lane to the village, his breath silver in the moonlight. If he was lucky, Tilly would be there at her grandmother's house. If she wasn't, he would leave a note. Either way, he would be seeing her soon enough. He didn't mind a wait. He'd got used to that over the weeks of his escape.

As he breathed in the crisp, clear air, and looked up at thousands of bright stars in the sky, it really hit him. He thought back to his early days in Kirkstead, back in the late summer, when he was convinced he would never see his eighteenth birthday, let alone Christmas. He had been wrong. Here he was, thinking, breathing, *existing*. He had lived where others had died and the future was still his.

Co-pilot:
2nd Lt Curtis Stearley

Pilot:
Captain Bob Holberg

Navigator:
2nd Lt Warren Cain

Engineer:
2nd Lt Ray LaFitte

Radio operator:
Sgt Clifford Skaggs

Bombardier:
2nd Lt Howard Bortz

B-17 *MACEY MAY* and her crew

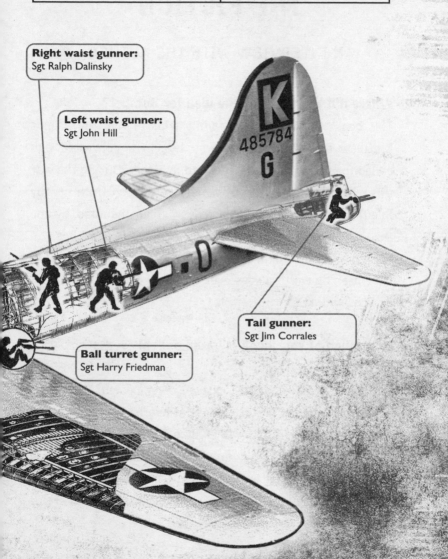

BOEING FLYING FORTRESS B-17 G

Engines: Four 1,200 hp Wright Cyclones	Height: 19 ft 1 in
Wing Span: 103 ft 9 in	Top Speed: Over 300 mph
Length: 74 ft 9 in	Service Ceiling: Over 35,600 feet

Right waist gunner:
Sgt Ralph Dalinsky

Left waist gunner:
Sgt John Hill

Tail gunner:
Sgt Jim Corrales

Ball turret gunner:
Sgt Harry Friedman

FACT BEHIND
THE FICTION

AN INTERVIEW WITH THE AUTHOR

Where did you first get the idea for Bomber?

This book was inspired by family trips to visit my friends Matthew and Julia Ward, who live in a converted pub called the Green Man in Kirkstead, Norfolk. During the war this pub was frequented by American airmen from nearby Seething airbase. Whenever I visit, I am haunted by the thought of these young men drinking their 'warm' beer on the nights before their bombing missions, when many would have been blown to pieces over places like Berlin, Stuttgart or Schweinfurt.

How much of your book is based on real events and places?

The planes and airbase at Kirkstead never existed, although it is loosely modelled on the airbase at nearby Seething, which was home to Liberators rather than Flying Fortresses. I do like to weave real history around the fictional characters in my books. The raids on Schweinfurt on August 17, 1943, and October 14, 1943, are based on actual USAAF raids on that city on those days. The departure of *Kansas Kate* from Kirkstead echoes the famous story of the *Memphis*

Belle, whose crew were lionised by the American media when they completed their twenty-five missions in 1943. Also, the passage in the book where *Macey May*'s chief mechanic Ernie Benik discovers a note from slave workers inside a dud German cannon shell in the wing of their B-17 is also based on real events.

What inspired you to write about a B-17?

The B-17 Flying Fortress is a fascinating aircraft. Although it had a reputation for toughness and durability, it never quite lived up to its name. Of the 12,731 B-17s built between 1936 and 1945, 4,754 were lost in action. Over 1943, when casualties in the air war were at their highest, it has been estimated that a Flying Fortress crew had a one in four chance of completing their twenty-five mission tour. Not all of the ten man crew would be killed, of course. Many airmen parachuted to safety, but those are still daunting odds.

Also, undeniably, the B-17's art deco curves made it one of the most beautiful aircraft of the Second World War. Some B-17s can still be seen in museums in Europe and America, and a few are still flying.

Are any of the characters based on real people?

All my main characters are fictitious although I have tried to reflect as accurately as I can the thoughts and experiences of the United States Eighth Air Force crews in 1943, and the extraordinarily brave members of the French Resistance. I often feel grateful I have never had to conjure the reserves of courage required by the characters in my novels.

A few of the senior figures featured here, such as General Eaker and 'Bomber' Harris, are real people, and some of the incidents between the characters in this book were inspired by real events and reported conversations. For example, the *Macey May* crew's conversation in the Green Man pub with the British pilots Gordon and Ray was inspired by a passage in Patrick Bishop's book *Bomber Boys*. The American journalist Eddie Burnet is fictitious, but the incident in which he features was inspired by the death of a *Life* magazine journalist who was killed while flying with the USAAF over Germany.

How did you research this book?

I like to walk the same streets as my characters, so wherever possible I visit the places where I set my stories. The couple of hours I spent at Seething airfield were invaluable. I also went to the RAF Museum in Hendon, London, to spend a fascinating afternoon with my agent Charlie Viney. I watched the 1949 film *Twelve O'Clock High*, starring Gregory Peck, to try to get a feel for how American airmen spoke, and also scores of videos on YouTube, and read many books about the air war over Europe, and the French Resistance escape routes used by downed Allied pilots.

ACKNOWLEDGEMENTS

Special thanks to Matthew and Julia Ward. On my last visit to their home in Kirkstead, Matthew took me to visit nearby Seething Control Tower Museum, where Jim Turner and his colleagues kindly allowed us to wander round, despite the tower being closed for maintenance. Do have a look at this website – www.seethingtower.org – and indeed, visit the museum if you are close by.

Thank you also to Patricia Everson, who very kindly agreed to talk to me at very short notice, and allowed me to look through her archive of photographs of Seething Air Base.

Thank you to my publisher, Ele Fountain, and my agent, Charlie Viney, who encouraged me to write this story, and my editor, Isabel Ford, who painstakingly moulded and polished these words with patience and perspicacity. Thanks also to Talya Baker, who copy-edited, Nick de Somogyi, who proofread, and James Fraser for his magnificent cover. And, as ever, Dilys Dowswell for her helpful comments on my first draft and Jenny and Josie Dowswell, who look after me and put up with my absences and odd hours.

NAIL-BITING TENSION, HEART-RACING

'A heart-stopping read'
SUNDAY TELEGRAPH

WINNER OF THE YOUNG QUILLS AWARD 2013

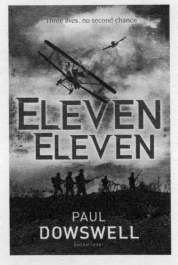

'With every turn of the page readers will hold their breath'
SCOTSMAN

ACTION ... FROM **PAUL DOWSWELL**

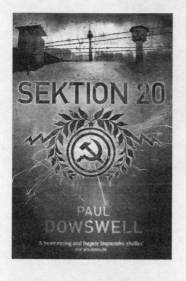

WINNER OF THE YOUNG QUILLS AWARD 2012

'A great thriller ... terrific'
BOOKSELLER

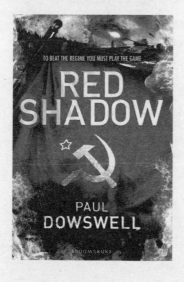

'A brilliant historical novelist'
SUNDAY TELEGRAPH

PAUL DOWSWELL is a prize-winning author of historical fiction. Among other awards he has twice won the Historical Association Young Quills Award, and also the Hamelin Associazione Culturale Book Prize, and for non-fiction the Rhône-Poulenc Junior Prize for Science Books. Paul is a frequent visitor to schools both in the UK and abroad, where he takes creative-writing classes and gives illustrated talks about his books. Away from work he enjoys travelling with his family, and playing with his band in the clubs and pubs of the West Midlands.

www.pauldowswell.co.uk